Xander

A Dark Assassins Novel
Book Three

Valerie Ullmer

Xander (A Dark Assassins Novel Book Three)

Copyright © 2017 Valerie Ullmer

This book is a work of fiction and any resemblance to persons, living or dead, places and locales, or events, is purely coincidental. All characters and events portrayed in this book are completely fictitious and dreamed up by the author.

Cover Design by Melody Simmons

Copy Edit by Faith Williams from The Atwater Group

DEDICATION

To all the books I've read and loved.

Chapter One

Xander

Xander glanced up from the thriller he was reading when he'd heard the sound of car tires turning onto his driveway, realizing that time had gotten away from him. Gunnar and Kane were coming over for weapons training Ghost had scheduled on New Year's Day, for a reason that escaped all three of them. Xander had designed and built the gun range deep into the woods behind his newly completed house and Ghost had designated it the training center for all of the assassins. And he couldn't fault Ghost for wanting his assassins to train. There had been another threat to Dark Company that Ghost had downplayed, not giving any of them details, but Xander could tell that he'd worried about it.

Besides, Xander had bought a Sig Sauer P226 over the holidays and it would be his first chance to test it out. And although he would never admit it aloud, he was grateful for the company so soon after the holidays.

Seth and Aubrey had gotten married back in November and although he was happy for them, and for Kai and Liv, and Reaper and Ara, he felt the stark loneliness acutely. Shaking off his melancholy, he opened the door. But before he could greet them, the three of them froze. They could hear the distinct crunching of snow and pine needles under heavy boots.

"About two miles north. Are you expecting anyone else?" Gunnar asked.

"No." Xander closed the door behind him and engaged the lock before he followed the other two as they moved toward the sound at a quick clip. He hadn't even bothered to grab a coat, but the snow and cold barely registered, even in his thin pullover and jeans. At least he had his shoes on before his friends arrived.

His eyes searched for movement, sensing the other two close, as they approached the origin of the sounds.

"I hear seven different strides…no, wait, make that eight. The last one has a lighter footfall than the others. Woman, possibly?"

That was when they heard the sound of metal slapping against a palm, as if they were getting ready to fire a gun.

Split up and we'll surround them. He used their mind link so no one could overhear their conversation.

Gunnar and Kane met his eyes and nodded, once, before they disappeared into the pines.

Xander heard the distinct steps, those trudging through the knee-deep mountain snow at an almost prohibitive pace, grunting as they grew tired from their trek. He knew that if they engaged them, the assassins would have the advantage of stealth, along with their ability to move freely.

Got eyes?

Xander received a flash of an image. Kane had gone for higher ground and had a view from miles around.

Yeah, on three of them. Dressed in white camo. They don't seem very coordinated and they are dragging the barrels of their AR-15s through the snow. Dumbasses. Xander heard Kane's sarcasm and bit back a laugh.

Then he heard from Gunnar. He and Jade were the best trackers he knew. *I got the others. There's a smaller figure, but whoever it is, their features are obscured by a hood and bulky jacket. That one doesn't have a weapon.*

Another image flashed and this one showed the clearing where the entire group sprawled out without any thought to formation or protection. Some had guns strapped to their backs; others held the guns loosely in their hands, unprepared to shoot at any sound or movement.

Xander soon moved into position and had eyes on them. He spotted an older man with short cropped, dark hair sprinkled with gray as he turned toward the small figure Gunnar spoke about.

"What animals made those tracks?"

Xander rolled his eyes. The snow was too deep for any definitive answer. It could have been anything from a bear to a fucking moose. He paused to hear the answer, but the mumble that came did nothing to clarify who the person was with these armed men. But something clicked and it made perfect sense.

I think they are looking for us. They have magazines clipped to their belts, handguns within easy reach, and knives for hand-to-hand combat. They are looking for animal tracks, and they are way too fucking close to where Reaper, Kai, Seth, and I have houses. There's nothing else up here that they could be searching for.

Xander froze when he heard a feminine voice carry over to him. She sounded closer than she had been even a few moments before. He should have sensed her coming closer. But the only question on his mind was why the fuck she was tagging along with a group of mercenaries. He heard the voice again, a tinny version of her voice, and for a long moment he couldn't understand the words. Until she stepped forward.

No, no. Not that way. Not that way.

Something warmed his chest as he heard her in his head as clearly as if they were speaking aloud. A familiarity washed over him and he felt connected to this woman in an elemental way. A feeling of a peace settled over him. He knew this was the first time he'd ever heard her voice. He was so stunned and happy that he didn't even question how they were able to mind link.

Can either of you hear the woman's thoughts?

Woman? Gunnar sounded confused.

Kane's reply was quick and clipped. *No.*

Hello?

Hello?

Xander tried to get her attention. *Can you hear me?*

He held his breath when he heard her distinct gasp, knowing that their mind link worked. His chest filled with dread at the thought that she gave herself away, until he heard her next words.

"I spotted a grizzly bear in the trees to the west. Sorry, I startled him and he ran off."

For long seconds, the men in the clearing stared at the woman before they were ordered to keep searching.

Xander stood close enough that he could see her curves underneath the heavy white parka. And having the worst timing in the world, Xander felt himself harden. He took a deep, cleansing breath of sharp mountain air that instantly cooled his overheated body.

Yes, I can hear you. These men, seven in total, are looking for immortals. They have been contracted by my boss at US Fish and Wildlife to kill them. Apparently the immortals are supposed to become animals. Can you help me without hurting yourself? They are heavily armed.

Xander was taken completely by surprise. She didn't question their connection but instead relayed vital information that he would need. He could also start to feel her emotions. She wasn't scared, just determined. He could hear her heart beating at a fast rate and her breathing strained from either the hike up the mountain or the tension in the air. He watched as she subtly shifted her head around as she searched for him, unable to spot him in the trees.

We can help. I'm going to communicate with my team and we'll take out the men. Are you okay with that?

Yes. I know they are paid mercenaries and I'm pissed that they killed a wolf two days ago for no other reason than they wanted to shoot something.

What's your name?

Frost.

Frost, I'm Xander. When I tell you to run, run south. Okay?

Yes, I understand.

Xander relayed the conversation he had with Frost. *We are going to have to kill them, there's no other way around it.* They couldn't have a threat looming over them, especially if one escaped and brought in a stronger, more trained group of mercenaries. Although they could easily defeat any group of fighters, keeping their existence a secret was crucial. The more humans who knew about them, the bigger the danger it posed.

Working as a team, they closed in on the unsuspecting mercenaries. At first, they quietly removed those men who were stationed on the outer perimeter, using knives to subdue them, or in Xander's case, using his bare hands and quickly snapping their necks. He didn't want Frost to see blood on him. The only sound he could detect was the grunts of the men who were dispatched. By the time Gunnar, Kane, and he closed in on their ranks, there were only three mercenaries remaining.

The older man spotted movement in Gunnar's direction and without hesitation raised his weapon and started to fire. The wolf easily dodged the shots before melting farther into the trees. Silence descended upon the area as the man searched for Gunnar.

Frost, run south. Keep as low as you can and use the trees as cover.

Gunnar emerged from the trees in order to distract those left alive and to provide additional cover. He fired at the mercenary closest to him, who had managed to roll away before he fired twice into Gunnar's chest at close range. The wolf shifter just grunted as the rounds struck. In the next instant, he shifted into his gray wolf form and lunged for the man, gripping his arm with his sharp teeth, and flung the man back and forth like a rag doll. After a few seconds, Gunnar had finished playing with his target and slammed him against the tree, effectively breaking his neck.

Kane darted forward and with one punch, crushed the other man's throat, effectively eliminating the second of the three.

One left.

His friends had taken care of the humans within seconds of hearing Xander's demand. He never took his eyes off Frost as she tried to run, but Xander noticed when she became distracted by Gunnar and watched as he shifted. On top of the distraction, she had to wade through knee-high snow in the thick winter gear that weighed her down, and she hadn't made it a few feet before he rushed toward her. Not waiting for the man to target Frost, Xander shifted into his snow leopard form and placed his body between Frost and the older mercenary.

The man froze, his arm straight out in front of him with his finger on the trigger. Xander could see that his pupils were blown and he was shaking in fear. Not lessening the tension, Xander lowered his furry head and raised his lips to show his long, sharp teeth ready to tear him apart limb from limb. He chuffed when he heard the man's heart quicken in fear.

The gunman snapped out of his stupor when he heard movement from Gunnar and Kane closing in on him; he quickly raised his semi-automatic and fired several rounds. Xander darted forward, taking a couple of rounds to his chest that didn't stop his momentum. But before he could reach the man, he heard a grunt of pain behind him. He turned in time to see her blood splash against the tree in front of her; she had turned to run during Xander's shift but a bullet had caught her in the back and passed through her right shoulder and out. As if in slow motion, he watched as she sank to her knees, clutching her wound.

His breath stuck in his throat and it felt as though his heart stopped.

Rage rushed through him when he heard the recognizable sound of the magazine being discharged and reloaded. He turned and the sight of his face twisted in fury must've been a horrifying sight, because the man paled and fumbled with the reload, forgetting completely about his sidearm. Not giving him a chance to remember, Xander leapt forward and opened his mouth around the man's neck as he landed with measured precision. With a quick tilt of his head, the man's neck snapped and Xander dropped him to the ground, forgotten.

He heard Kane snarl and Gunnar let out a howl, but Xander ran toward Frost. She had managed to sit up and lean back against the tree nearest to where she fell, her bright-red blood unnatural against the stark white of her parka and the snow that surrounded them. Her eyes widened when she took in the snow leopard that loped toward her. Without fear, she reached out with her left hand, asking silently for permission to touch him. He lowered his head and moved his lips over his teeth, not wanting to scare her. When her fingers ran through his white fur, he purred when her touch electrified his body.

"You're beautiful." Her eyes widened as she turned her gaze to the gigantic gray wolf that sauntered over with blood on his muzzle. "Wow, you too."

She tried to sit up and lean forward, but instead her movement caused a hiss of pain to escape her throat. "Well...shit. I was kinda hoping to avoid getting shot by those trigger-happy fuckers. I'll just have to try harder the next time I'm forced to track immortals so they could be eliminated. Oh, wait, there won't be a next time because they are dead."

Xander shivered at the look of glee that sparked in her bright-green eyes as Kane laughed and Gunnar let out a low growl. Then Xander noticed that her eyes were more than green. There was a light-blue crescent, similar to the color of his eyes, that blended easily into the green. He shook off his thoughts when she flinched in pain and shifted back. He noted that her eyes widened as she roamed over his naked form, but after a minute, her eyes darted back to his sure to be amused ones.

"Are you Xander? The one I've been talking to in my...well...mind, I guess you could say?"

He nodded as he moved forward, taking her left hand in both of his.

"I really was trying to lead them away, but despite me trying to convince them that they were headed in the wrong direction, they noticed the smaller animals avoiding this area. All animals will always listen to their instincts and stay away from apex predators." She paused for a long moment, her eyes never leaving his as she explained. "Sorry, I tend to talk a lot when I'm in pain...or nervous. But I got shot in the shoulder and it hurts like hell."

Xander and Kane chuckled, bringing out a huge smile on Frost's face.

"There you go. You guys looked so serious for a minute. But seriously, the cold is helping, but my ass is starting to go numb. You don't talk much, do you? Well, I ramble so that's why I became a wildlife biologist. So I can talk to the animals instead of getting weird looks from people. If I didn't see him in his human form, I could've sworn the gray wolf thought I was crazy. Although, animals give me about the same confused looks that you guys are giving me now. Huh."

Xander couldn't tear his eyes away from her.

"Are you sure she was shot? She's not really acting like it," Kane said.

Frost pulled her gaze away from Xander and glanced up, way up, to where Kane stood with his arms crossed, wearing a short-sleeved shirt and jeans with just a pair of tennis shoes on. Xander could tell that her pulse didn't increase, nor did her pupils widen, as she glanced at Kane. He relaxed until her eyes narrowed a fraction.

"And what do you know about it, Blondie?"

Kane raised one of his eyebrows, too stunned to talk.

"I've been running on adrenaline for the past few days, trying to lead these assholes off a cliff while avoiding any evidence I found of animals in the area, but there isn't a cliff around here that is hidden. So how about we cut me some slack?"

Xander jerked out of his astonishment when she tried to stand. As she spoke to Kane, he traced every inch of her. Beautiful pale skin, plump peach lips, beautiful green-blue eyes, and long, flowing dark hair. But her cry as her movement pulled at her wound had him darting forward, wrapping his arm around her waist and pulling her close. The humming that he hadn't recognized before faded away abruptly when he touched Frost. She seemed to sense the silence and comfort as well, because she sagged against him, blowing out a relieved breath.

Should I get Liv? Gunnar communicated while still in wolf form.

"Can you point me to the nearest hospital?" Frost grunted with her face pinched in pain.

"No." Xander's fierce anger came out of his mouth, before he realized that the harshness might have Frost fear him. Instead, she smiled.

"Yes, Gunnar, can you go and get Liv?" The wolf ran off through the trees as soon as Xander spoke.

Xander lifted her in his arms and walked toward his house, taking care not to jar her too much. But when he spotted a cringe with each step, he cradled her in his arms and it managed to lessen the shock.

"Who's Liv? Your wife? A doctor?"

Xander's heart ran a mile a minute because he knew that after searching for years, decades even, that he'd finally found his mate. And she was tough, beautiful, and brilliant. He held her tighter to his body when he started to salivate, already feeling the need to claim her. But putting his selfish needs on hold, he cursed himself because he wasn't able to protect her.

"No, Liv's a friend and a vampire. Kai is her husband and mate."

Frost relaxed in his arms and he continued to explain.

"The blond is Kane—he's also a vampire. Gunnar is a gray wolf shifter, as you saw."

"And you're Xander, who I can somehow communicate with through my mind. Which is completely wicked, by the way."

He laughed, cutting off the sound, not wanting to jostle her too much. "Yes, and I'm a snow leopard."

"Huh."

He glanced down and met her gaze, his eyebrow lifted in a question.

"Well, snow leopards aren't native to Colorado, but since you're a shifter, it doesn't really matter. Hell, I didn't know that vampires existed outside the teen romance vampire books. Which I'm not admitting that I read. But I did." She winked at him.

He smiled and held her close. "There are several vampires and shifters around."

"And they all live in Snowfall?"

"Most of us do."

"But why Snowfall? Oh, are all of you in the same profession?

Please don't say forest rangers."

Xander laughed. "No, we're government assassins."

Frost had gone quiet and when he glanced down, her brows were lowered in thought for long minutes before she spoke. "That's how you were able to take care of those men so easily. I'm glad I ran into you."

As the house came into view, Frost glanced up and her eyes widened as she surveyed the massive structure. She darted a glance behind his shoulder and cringed. "Sorry I brought them so close to your house."

"It's not your fault. You didn't know. I take it you didn't volunteer to lead them?"

Frost scoffed. "No. My boss, that asshole, told the mercenaries that I was the best tracker they had. I mean, come on, mercenaries? Another group I had no idea really existed until three days ago. When I found out what he hired them for, I figured the only way to save humans and animals from being slaughtered was to lead the expedition, but away from anyone they could harm. I tried to steer them farther up the mountain, but they became impatient after two days of spotting nothing and started their own way. If you hadn't come across us when you did, I was afraid that they would've started killing randomly. I wonder why my boss wanted to kill you and your friends?"

"Your boss is probably the middleman. Dark Company is very lucrative and it's only because we're trained and very successful at what we do. Anytime there's money or power involved, someone will try to make a grab for it. It's not the first time, and it won't be the last."

"When the leader, the one who shot me, doesn't call to check in, they'll send another group to the last known GPS location. He makes the call at ten every night."

They reached Xander's front door and he grabbed the spare key in a hiding spot beside the door, all while glancing at her face for any signs of pain. Making sure not to jostle her, he pushed it open. He turned toward the living room. His plan was to lay her on the couch, but as he leaned down, she balked.

"I would prefer to sit somewhere the blood won't stain your furniture."

"It's comfortable and I can always get another couch."

"No, don't worry about my comfort. I've had worse. The bathroom is fine."

"What?"

Frost blushed and looked down. "Early on in my career, I was attacked by a mountain lion. I had been tracking a bear cub who had broken his leg and I wasn't paying close attention to my surroundings or the direction I headed. The mountain lion pounced and caught me on the side with his claw, before something scared him away. That hurt worse than getting shot."

She had spoken easily about a wound that might have killed her, and he had been so stunned by the matter-of-fact delivery, that he moved toward the bathroom before he could process what he was doing. He gently lowered her onto the bench in the shower, grateful that it was large enough to cradle her body.

Frost's face pinched in pain and he silently called for Liv to hurry. To distract both of them, he kept asking her questions as he removed her outerwear and sweater carefully, leaving her in a long-sleeved shirt and jeans.

"Why did your parents name you Frost?"

She laughed and something inside him bloomed at the light and infectious sound.

"My mother loves everything about winter. But I was the opposite of what she expected. They both have light, almost white hair, like yours. They have pale skin and light-blue eyes. And of course when I was born, I had a full head of black hair, and while I do have pale skin, my eyes are green. My mother loves that I'm different. I'm twenty-seven, with no prospects to even think about getting married and I work with animals. She worries about me, but she's given up on thinking I'll do anything normal."

He smoothed his hand down her black hair and she leaned into his hand. He smiled knowing that she trusted him.

Before they could continue the conversation, he heard Liv's tiny footsteps as she rushed up his staircase. She rushed into the bathroom and directly into the shower stall where Frost struggled to sit up the moment she spotted the tiny vampire in the room. Xander propped her up on the bench as she stared at the small, curly-haired vampire who came to a stop inches in front of her face. Xander shook his head as he watched Kai, Gunnar, Kane, Seth, and Jade rush into the already crowded room.

Frost's movements had slowed significantly, but when she spotted Jade trail after the others, a low growl erupted from her throat. When Jade stepped forward, Frost erupted with a more animalistic growl that had Jade take a step back and hold her hands out in front of her. Frost's eyes never left the red fox, but Jade made the mistake of glancing over to Xander before she took a tentative step forward.

"Get the fuck away from Xander, before I rip your head off."

The room stilled at the threat, and for the first time since he'd known her, Xander could see actual fear reflected in Jade's eyes.

Xander stepped closer to Frost and felt her entire body relax. But he could see that the tension in her body caused her to bleed profusely. He knew that he needed to get Jade out of the room before Frost went critical, but when he said Jade's name, he realized his mistake at once. A loud roar, the sound almost deafening, erupted throughout the room. Disregarding her injury, Frost stepped in front of Xander and bared her teeth at Jade.

Before Jade could leave or Frost could attack, Liv stepped in Frost's view, despite Kai's protesting snarl. Instead of pushing Liv out of the way and attacking, Frost slumped back against Xander and he wrapped his arms around her to pull her closer.

Xander could spot the anger in Liv's eyes as she glanced up at him.

"You haven't explained it to her yet?"

Xander shook his head, not sure in Frost's condition that she was ready to hear about their connection.

Liv turned her gaze to the woman in front of her. "I'm sorry, honey. I didn't catch your name."

"I'm Frost, and you're beautiful. Are you Liv?" Frost's voice sounded strained.

"Yes, I'm Liv. Do you remember what happened to you?" While she asked her questions, Liv reached for the hem of Frost's shirt. Moving faster than either he or Liv thought possible, Frost jerked back out of Liv's reach and to Xander's surprise, forced him back as well.

"Not the shirt. You can rip off the sleeve, but I'm not taking it off."

Liv nodded and without hesitation, ripped the right shirt sleeve off and examined the wound. She pressed a clean bandage against her wound on both sides, and flinched as Frost screamed before biting her lower lip.

"Do you mind if Seth draws some blood?"

She shook her head. Her lids were slower as they blinked up and down.

Seth darted to Frost's side and she blinked at him before he smiled. "You're fast. Oh, right, immortal. I keep forgetting."

After Seth made quick work of the blood, Liv removed the bandage and examined the bullet wound, which exited the front. Tears formed in Liv's eyes, and then in Seth's, while the others in the room took a gasping breath.

"It's okay. I'm okay. It's nothing. I won't need surgery, especially with the range of motion I still have. So if you just sew me up, I would appreciate it."

Xander couldn't believe how Frost was able to deal with the pain, as if it were nothing. But when Liv pressed a clean bandage around the leaking wound, the pain and exhaustion caught up with her. With a moan, Frost's eyes fluttered closed and she passed out in his arms. He moved to lay her on the bench and without realizing it, his movements caused her shirt to ride up and expose her old wound to their view. It looked as though a chunk of her side was missing. When he glanced closer, he could see claw marks.

Xander's throat clogged with emotion, taking the time to brush her hair out of her face, before he placed chaste kisses on her face. When he pressed one last kiss to her lips, unable to stay away not that he'd found her, he could've sworn that she kissed him back. Her breathing was even, although it hitched every once in a while, as Liv made quick work of cleaning the wound, before she stitched it and dressed both the entrance and exit wound.

When Liv indicated that she had finished, he lifted Frost in his arms and gently laid her on the bed.

"Xander?" Liv's voice was tight, but she wanted to know.

"She was mauled by a mountain lion several years ago. And tonight, I wasn't fast enough to stop her from getting shot." As he ran his hand down his face, blowing out a frustrated sigh, he realized that his words were met with complete silence.

Chapter Two

Frost

Consciousness sucked. The intense fire that scorched her from the inside out spread slowly through her body. The worst of the burning, and what had woken her, was the scorching sensation on the soles of her feet and it had continued upward. It was now at her thighs, licking up to her hips, and she wondered whether she were truly on fire. She rolled her eyes under her closed lids at her dumbass thought. She had been unable to pry them open no matter how hard she'd tried.

Panic sounded like a solid plan, but whenever she tensed her body, her throat would clog and the fire would only intensify, so she cursed her reflexes as she unlocked her muscles, one area at a time. When she was able to breathe normally, or as normal as her situation allowed her to, she had a chance to take stock of the situation.

She concentrated on the pain first. Her wounded shoulder, the surge of pain that she remembered before she blacked out into nothingness, was there, but the throb was minor compared to the burning sensations that were getting closer to her navel. In addition to the burning, there was an underlying ache that encompassed her entire being. It compared to the flu, but only by a little. This time, the pain brought tears to her eyes.

Her high tolerance for pain deserted her at this moment, and she sought relief in any form she could get it. She couldn't open her eyes, so she tried swallowing to check whether her throat worked, but she couldn't move to even do that. She tried to groan or shout, any vocalization that she could think of, to beg for any pain medication that would get rid of this torture she was going through, but no sound escaped.

Xander.

Once she thought of the beautiful, muscular man with bright-white hair and penetrating blue eyes, she forced herself to take slow, deep breaths, relaxing her muscles to at least unclench her jaw. It did nothing but add more pain to her already strained body, and she didn't know whether she was grateful or mad at herself as she let the blackness overwhelm her.

***

The next time she awoke, she immediately thought of the throbbing fire that had struck her body so fiercely that last time. For a split second, she thought they might have passed, but the fire still licked her body and her bones ached even worse than before. And on top of that, she had a splitting headache that made her feel sick to her stomach.

She thought that she heard her name, but she couldn't be certain because the voice sounded distant. She couldn't identify the gender of the speaker. Once again, she tried to open her eyes, but found herself unable. With force and concentration, she was able to open her chapped lips a fraction, but as she tried to push words through her throat, the only thing that sounded in her ears was a whimper.

Her body locked down when she heard the rustle of sheets next to her head, and she relaxed as she thought about Xander. *Was he okay?* She remembered the pain etched on his face as he laid her down on his bed. She was able to fight consciousness long enough to see the guilt reflected in his eyes, but for the life of her, she couldn't reassure him. She did feel the press of his lips against hers, but that memory might have been a dream because she had wanted it so badly. But she wanted to ask him why he had that look on his face, and she wanted to figure out why it bothered her so much to see him in pain.

The first time she heard his clear voice inside her head, she felt a sense of peace wash over her that she'd never experienced before. Although any other time, hearing a stranger's voice so intimately would have freaked her out. But with Xander, it felt natural. And when he came into view, she couldn't look away from his gaze. Only when he turned to confront the mercenaries did her eyes move to the exposed olive skin on his arms, his huge stature, and beautiful white hair that added to his attractiveness, if that was even possible. He was powerful and massive, compared to most other men she'd seen. And the sheer power that he exuded had her shiver with a need she'd never thought herself capable of.

Frost had no idea with their connection meant, but logic bullied its way to the forefront of her mind. He must've been nice to her because she'd been hurt. No man who looked like Xander, and who radiated power and control, would ever fall for a curvy woman who had found herself comfortable with animals, not humans.

And then she had to be snarky to the tall blond Xander had indicated was Kane, the vampire. Then she didn't shut up the entire time in the woods, talking about fuck only knows what. She had felt so out of control of the situation that her mouth ran without forming a single thought in her mind. She had tried to avoid thinking about it, but the violent way she reacted to the redhead Xander had called Jade made her feel worse than the pains that throbbed throughout her body. She had almost attacked an innocent woman with no other cause than she walked into the bathroom.

Frost's thought paused for a moment when her body was doused in cold. The heat dissipated and with it, the extreme ache of her bones lessened slightly, and she blew out a relieved breath. Again, she tried to open her eyes or at least thank whoever had relieved the pain, but her body sank into the mattress and she found herself being pulled into the darkness of sleep.

***

Awareness came slowly this time. At first she had become aware of Xander's scent, somewhere close. And then, she heard several voices close by. Xander's voice sounded worried, anxious, and she couldn't understand why. She must've scrunched her brows because as his voice drew closer to her, he carefully touched her forehead with his wonderfully cool fingers, and she blew out a sigh at the sensation. When she felt a brush of a kiss against her mouth, a different throb had overtaken her body and she tilted her head back to get closer to Xander's lips. She still couldn't speak; she tried. She wanted to beg Xander to relieve this new ache as it throbbed in her core and steadily spread, but his hand paused on her cheek.

Xander's voice cut off, not that she could understand a word he spoke. She cursed her body's reaction to his touch when he pulled his hand away from her skin. She missed him and his touch acutely. For the longest time, she strained to hear anyone who could be near, cursing that she was trapped in the abyss of her mind. When her body tired from the strain of her awareness of those around her and when she almost faded out again, she heard Xander speak to her.

Despite her attention focused on him and the sound of his voice, she couldn't understand what he tried to convey to her. Her brows drew down, and she was a little surprised by the movement, but most of her craved to know what Xander wanted to say to her.

Xander's tone became excited after her tiny movement, but she scrunched her eyelids closed and concentrated on the words. Finally, she thought she could hear her name as he spoke. She sighed in relief when Xander slid her hand in his and linked their fingers together. But again, his touch had her body throbbing. Not from pain, but pleasure. She scoffed at herself for her horrendous timing, but she wondered how her shifter would react. Slowly and painstakingly, she forced her eyes open, only to find a concerned Xander staring at her.

His eyes were rimmed in red and his beautiful hair stood on end, as if he'd been constantly running his hands through it.

"Do you know what's happening?" Xander's voice sounded low and scratchy.

She managed to shake her head, only small movements, twice.

"You passed out when Liv touched your wound and when I caught you, I pressed a kiss to your lips. I needed to feel close to you and offer you some comfort. But I didn't expect you to respond."

It hadn't been a dream. She forced herself to think back to those moments that were fuzzy from the extreme amount of pain and throbbing from her shoulder, and she distinctly remembered the cool lips that pressed to hers, and the resulting tingle that spread from her lips. She wanted to feel the kiss again, to burrow into Xander until the pain ebbed, but her thoughts became muddled.

"Liv believes that our kiss started your transition from human to shifter. She has tested your blood and found that you already had shifter DNA. Your body recognized my touch and accepted me as your mate when we kissed, which started the transition."

Thinking that she was too weak to speak, she tried to use their mind link that she shared with him earlier, but her body and her thoughts were too weak to complete it.

"Mate?" She flinched at the sound of her own voice.

"Yes, sweetheart. I've been waiting a long time for you."

"Y' too. Tired."

"Your transition is almost complete and the next time you wake, you'll be stronger, with no effects of the gunshot wound or the pain that you had to go through while you changed. Don't worry, sweetheart, I won't leave you."

His reassurance had the tension melting from her body and she smiled against his lips as he gave her a brief kiss. *I hope you're right. Next time I kiss him, I will be completely aware of it.*

***

She blinked open her eyes and glanced around to get a sense of her surroundings in the semi-darkness of the room. She took a deep breath, but she didn't recognize the scents that assailed her. It was oddly comforting—a mix of grapefruit, mint, and vanilla—and she took another cleansing breath, memorizing the scent for future reference.

Tempting fate and hoping there would be no pain, she pointed her toes as she stretched her calves. She blew out a breath when nothing hurt at her movement. She tried her arms next, lifting them above her head and stretching. Again, no pain and her muscles loosened with every movement.

As she moved, she realized that her hair felt limp and greasy and the shirt that clung to her felt stiff and unclean. Ready for a shower, she glanced around the room and noticed details that she'd never before been able to do. But before she could investigate or find a bathroom in order to take a long shower, someone next to her took a deep breath.

She looked to her left and found Xander sleeping on his stomach, with his hands tucked underneath his head. His beautiful bronzed skin shone from the moonlight that filtered into the room. Unable to keep her hands to herself, she ran her fingers through his soft hair and listened to his sigh at her touch. He turned his head toward her and she could see the dark spots underneath his eyes as he slept soundly, his breathing deep and undisturbed. He must've gotten very little sleep during her transition, which, as she thought back on, seemed like weeks to her.

The thoughts of the heat that flashed over her body had her searching the room for the entrance to the bathroom. Taking care not to jostle Xander, she slid herself off the bed and wandered toward the bathroom. At the doorway, she glanced back and took a long look at her mate. Her heart beat hard in her chest at how much she loved the connection she had with Xander.

But would he want her because he believed her to be his mate? She would have never believed in immortals or believed that she was the mate of one before she met Xander, but she had seen the proof for herself. He had even managed to convince her of the truth in his words. But if he had been waiting for someone, his true mate, and he grew tired of waiting, could he have convinced himself that she was his mate because it was convenient?

She had literally brought danger to his doorstep, and even though she might not be his true mate, she could find out why her boss had hired the armed soldiers for rent and prevent him from sending another team. *If he hadn't done so already.*

At that last horrifying thought, she hurried through her shower. She loved that she was surrounded by his scent as she used his shampoo and soap, and despite her warnings to herself, she could feel her body responding. Up until now, she had never felt overtly sexual, but Xander's scent alone could send her into a tailspin of desire.

As she toweled off, she glanced in the mirror and glanced at the spot where a gunshot wound had been. She remembered that it hurt like crazy, but her skin was smooth at the spot, as though it never happened. Then she glanced down and winced.

Fuck, fate couldn't heal the gouges on my side?

Shaking her head with disgust, she wrapped the towel tightly around her torso and quietly made her way toward Xander's dresser, hoping that he wouldn't mind if she borrowed some clothes. She found a pair of sweats and a tee, both making her feel like a child as they dwarfed her, but they smelled like Xander. She breathed a sigh of relief when she glanced around the bedroom and found her bra on the arm of the chair and slipped it on.

Realizing her time with Xander had come to an end, she turned to look at Xander one last time. She hoped that they would cross paths someday.

Pain that she hadn't been expecting ripped through her chest as she neared the bedroom door. Her breath caught in her throat. But she knew that she had to draw danger away from him, and forced herself to open the door and walked through it.

The house was dark and quiet, and although she could visibly see what she couldn't as a human, she prevented herself from snooping as she walked through the house, toward the exit. Every part of her being screamed for her to be with Xander and she hesitated right before the front door. That hesitation lasted longer than she would have liked, and she forced herself forward despite the throbbing pain that screamed she was making a mistake. But the moment she touched the doorknob, she heard a low, menacing growl behind her and it stopped her movements.

She turned to face Xander. When she noticed the fierce look on his face, she flinched back against the door.

"Where the hell do you think you're going?"

She opened her mouth to explain, but when a small squeak escaped, she felt the blood rush to her cheeks and she snapped her mouth closed. Her eyes widened as she realized he stood in front of her naked. Unable to help herself, she allowed her eyes to roam over his naked form. Her core throbbed with need, but she remembered her manners and snapped her eyes back to meet his. She barely bit back a low groan of disgust at herself.

"Sorry." It sounded like a cross between a question and a statement and she flinched again.

"Are you apologizing for trying to leave or for looking at me naked?"

Instead of answering his question, she explained, "I have to stop my asshole of a boss from sending more mercenaries."

Her eyes widened as Xander stepped closer to her. "You're not leaving me, sweetheart. We will pay your boss a visit, but I want to have a chance to get to know you, and you to know me. I can't stand the thought of you leaving now that I've finally found you."

Frost knew then that his words were the truth. She was his mate that he'd been waiting years, or much longer, for and she was going to walk out on him without an explanation, knowing it would hurt him. *Well…fuck.*

"I'm sorry, Xander. I just wanted to protect you and the others."

"Will you give me, us, a chance?"

"Yes. I won't try to leave again."

This man was important to her, and now that the panic had left her mind, she realized that the pain in her chest was because she had almost left him. Her body was trying to tell her something that her heart already knew. She couldn't leave Xander.

She looked up at him when he cupped her cheek gently, and with a silent nod, he captured her lips and proceeded to kiss her breathless.

Chapter Three

Xander

Xander broke the kiss and held Frost close. His heart nearly beat out of his chest when he realized how close he was to having her walk out of his life. He could feel his body shaking because of it. The next time he saw Reaper, he was going to hug the man.

The transition had been just as harrowing as Reaper described, but what Xander dismissed was the pure helplessness he would feel at not being able to help your mate through the most painful experience of their life. And like Ara's transition, Frost was taken by surprise when she had begun her transition, without him having released his venom into her bloodstream or knowing that transitioning was a possibility.

It had been pure torture to watch Frost writhe in pain, especially considering her gunshot wound hadn't healed until the transition had been completed. And he watched her like a hawk for three days and three nights, trying to lessen the pain and prevent her from tearing the wound in her shoulder, as he tried to get her to sleep comfortably. Reaper's trick worked, setting the alarm for every half an hour to replace the wet towels he had surrounding her body. The first time he removed the towels, he had cursed at the heat that radiated from her skin, before making quick work of switching out the towels.

And because he refused to sleep during this, he had stupidly fallen asleep when he had been too exhausted to keep going, a few hours before she woke. When he had caught her scent mixed with his soap, he had shot up in bed and looked around for her. Panic set in when he couldn't spot her, but he heard her speaking softly to herself as she made her way downstairs, and shot out of bed to go after her.

When she turned to face him, his breath caught in his throat as he spotted the minor changes that the transition to shifter had made in her appearance. She was as beautiful as when he first spotted her in the clearing, and the transition had only enhanced her features. She stood straighter and looked stronger, with more defined muscles, as if she were ready to pounce at any moment. She was his mate and he'd finally found her after all this time.

He found that he couldn't stay away from her. When she tilted her head, he devoured her lips and lost himself in her touch for several long minutes. But a rash thought came to mind and he pulled away from the kiss.

"Have you shifted yet?"

She blinked once, and then again, before the question had sunk in and confusion became etched on her face. "No. I felt the need for a shower and all these thoughts bombarded me, but the only one I could pick out was finding my boss and kicking the little fucker in the balls. Why should I be able to shift now, when I wasn't able to before?"

"The only thing I can think of is that you transitioned with just a touch from your mate, so it could be that your ability to shift is repressed. Liv and the rest of the immortals don't really know the ins and outs of becoming an immortal. Why we are in a stasis and we are unable to age, or why some of us can shift quickly while others can't. There is so much unknown about us, and Liv had come to a standstill in her research before she tested your blood. All I know is that unless an immortal is trained to mind link with another immortal, which takes years to learn even if you've done it successfully before, an immortal can mind link with their mate if one of them accepts their connection. I knew the first time I heard your thoughts that you were my mate."

He watched as Frost's nose scrunched at his last statement. But before he could question it, she asked him a question.

"My shoulder wound healed because I transitioned?"

He nodded but he couldn't help but glance down at her side. He watched as her face twisted in horror.

"You…you saw?"

Xander was confused by her panic and pulled her closer. "It doesn't matter what it looks like. It shows everyone how strong you are and what you've gone through in your life. It's nothing to be ashamed of, sweetheart. I felt guilty when I saw it because you were shot due to my inability to protect you. I added to your pain. I know I should have protected you, gotten you to safety before the mercenary had a chance to take the shot, but my ego wouldn't allow me to walk away from the fight. You had to get hurt for me to realize how impulsive and stupid I was."

"It wasn't your fault."

He shook his head and held onto her tighter. "I don't think you'll ever win that argument with me."

She scoffed but relaxed in his arms.

"You are the most beautiful woman I've ever seen. I'm a lucky man."

"Yeah, right. The wound healed in a way that makes it look grotesque and even then, the rest of me isn't anything to look at either."

His lips slammed into hers and he growled as she opened for him. He slid his tongue inside, tasting her sweetness and loving the moans that he drew from her. He knew without a doubt that he was falling for this woman. "Never doubt my need and desire for you. You are gorgeous and you fit perfectly against me, and I will always want you. And I know that you were hoping that your old injury would heal because of the transition, but Liv and I think that transitions only heals fresh wounds."

He paused and her blue-green eyes were wide as she looked at him for an explanation.

"When Liv met Kai, her life had been in danger because she found out the company she worked for had created a deadly virus that killed immortals, which is next to impossible. She asked Kai for help, and he took her in and protected her. He knew long before he'd actually spoken to her that she was his mate, but he was in denial. So while she worked on the antidote, they got to know each other and fell in love. But Liv was kidnapped and beaten within an inch of her life—several broken bones, a head injury, and a stab wound to her side. Kai's venom healed her from her newly-inflicted wounds.

"Liv believes that your body had awhile to adapt to the old injury, and became part of you just as much as the color of your hair and eyes. This is just a theory on why your wound didn't heal during your transition. But, at this point, it's all a guessing game. Before you, it was unheard to transition without having venom in your system."

Xander had watched her as he explained and noticed that tears had welled in her eyes, and he pulled her close.

"Who would want to hurt Liv?"

"The scientist wanted to become an immortal and take over Dark Company, but Liv ruined that chance when she discovered his experiment and put a stop to it. He was also bat-shit crazy. Liv used the same bio-weapon he created against him, but in humans they just disintegrate until there's nothing left. But now Liv is happy, in love and married to her mate, and she keeps researching in case someone else develops a plan to come after us."

For a long moment, they were silent as Frost processed this new information. But he came to the sudden realization that he was still naked when he could feel the heat and smell the arousal coming from Frost. He reined in his desire and allowed himself a small kiss.

"You must be famished after not eating for close to four days. I'll go get dressed and cook us breakfast."

She nodded and he indicated where she could find the kitchen as he rushed upstairs and threw on a pair of baggy sweats and a tee.

When he arrived in the kitchen, Frost was glaring at the coffee maker, trying to figure out how it worked, and he brushed by her, placing a kiss on her head as he chuckled. Her hand shot out and she slugged him in the chest, before she stepped back and watched as Xander taught her how to use the machine.

As the first cup of coffee started to brew, he snagged a kiss, smiling against her mouth when she leaned into him. Not wanting to push her into anything until she was ready, he reluctantly stepped back and ended the kiss. He turned to hide his obvious reaction to her nearness by digging in the fridge and made quick work of cooking breakfast.

"How old are you?"

"Technically, I'm a hundred twenty-two, but physically, I look exactly as I did when I turned twenty-two and stopped aging."

"Did your mate turn you?"

"No, sweetheart, you're my mate. I was on a hunting trip with my father and older brothers, making sure that we had enough food to get through the winter, when I was separated from my family and attacked. As soon as I felt teeth pierce my shoulder, I passed out and woke up as a shifter."

"So, you don't remember anything about your transition? Not the heat or the pain?"

Xander couldn't help it; he flinched at the thought of Frost in pain. "No, I have no memories of that. I remember blood, but that could have been the pain or a false memory, but I don't remember anything until I awoke on the hard, snow-covered ground, alone."

"What happened to your family?"

Xander swallowed as he pulled up the horrific memories of what he found after he'd become a shifter. "I found my two older brothers dead from the same shifter attack. Dad made it home but when he spotted me, he wouldn't let me anywhere near the house, thinking that I had been the one who attacked my brothers. Instead of arguing, I let my parents be and left."

"How did you become an assassin?" She had finished her breakfast and thanked him. She sipped her coffee, looking at him with concern.

He laughed at the memory. "I ran into Kai one day while I was wandering around the mountains. I thought he was a threat, being a vampire and all, and I attacked him without thinking it through. We fought for close to an hour, and while I suspected then and now that he could easily kill me, he pulled his punches and kept his teeth retracted. Shifter venom is deadly to vampires, and vice versa. What I learned later was that Kai was almost a century older than me and had been working as an assassin, training all day every day for decades, so of course I ran out of steam and lost the fight. I expected him to kill me, but Kai had offered me a hand, lifted me off the ground, and took me to see Ghost for a job."

"You…mentioned that I'm your mate and you've been waiting for me. How do you know I'm the one for you?" Frost pulled her bottom lip in between her teeth and he groaned as lust surged through him.

"I had an inkling when I could hear your thoughts, but the moment I spotted you, every cell in my body screamed for me to protect you. To be honest, before I heard you, I thought I was destined to be alone. Kai found Liv close to four years ago, Reaper found Ara soon after, and even Seth, the kid, found his vampire mate, Aubrey, last year. She turned him in November and they married soon after. Out of everyone, I was the only one who had believed that mates were real and I desired to find you, but I lost hope until I heard your voice."

There was a pause as she absorbed all the information that he'd thrown at her, but he had to ask.

"How do you feel about becoming a shifter and finding out that you're my mate?"

"To be honest, the idea has settled into place with ease. I'd always felt out of place, preferring to be alone. Before I heard you, my thoughts were always so loud, rioting in my head, but they calmed the moment you spoke to me. I feel safe and comfortable with you, and I'm willing to accept the relationship, but I do have one question."

Choked by her easy acceptance, he nodded.

"Are you attracted to me or do you want to be with me because I'm your mate?"

"No, sweetheart. Everything about you attracts me—from the sound of your voice to the way your mouth quirks on one side when you're being sarcastic. How your eyes light up that particular shade of green when you're happy, or hungry, or thinking. You're beautiful on the outside as much as you radiate beauty on the inside. Even if my instincts, well, every part of my being didn't scream for you to be mine, I would still know that I belong to you."

Her hand cupped her throat with each word he spoke, and by the end, he reached toward her cheek and wiped a tear from her face. "Mates don't ever cheat, lie, or hurt each other. I would never do anything to make you stop believing that I want you every moment of every day."

Frost launched herself into his arms and proceeded to ravage his mouth, leaving his mind blank and his heart racing. He memorized every inch of her mouth and he pulled her onto his lap. Only when they needed to breathe, they broke apart and he pulled her close.

"If I'm a shifter now, why haven't I shifted?"

"I don't know. I have a feeling that you're unique and will shift in your own time. But if you're worried about it, we could talk to Liv and have her investigate."

She nodded. "I would like to find out, and I need to apologize to Jade and Kane. I still have no idea what came over me when I saw her."

"Well, you aren't the only one who's had that reaction to Jade. Ara had a panic attack when she thought that Jade and Reaper had a relationship. Liv had tried to walk away and ignore her jealousy, until we told her that shifters and vampires can't mate. Aubrey pulled Seth behind her when Jade had tried to hug him. She even released her fangs and snarled at her. You were injured and your instincts told you that I was important to you; that's why you reacted the way you did. Jade won't fault you for that."

Frost nodded and melted back against Xander. He couldn't get enough of her and he couldn't wipe the smile off his face. His mate was in his lap and had accepted him. And he would do everything in his power to keep her happy.

Chapter Four

Frost

Frost smiled and waved at the people she had gotten to know over the years she had worked at the US Department of Fish and Wildlife, loving the feeling of Xander walking next to her. His presence allowed her to project an air of nonchalance. She hated being in crowded areas, and downtown Denver had grown more and more crowded over the years. Too many people made her feel claustrophobic, which was why she preferred the outdoors.

"Do you live in the city?"

She shook her head. "I only come for monthly staff meetings. Well, I try to show up for them, but most of the time I make excuses that I'm tracking a particular species and I can't make it in without losing the trail. It's been several months, to be honest. I rent a small cabin in Snowfall and traveled wherever the job took me."

He smiled at her and she found herself returning the smile, not feeling at all self-conscious.

The one thing that she loved about being an immortal was the strength she could feel pulsing through her veins. Although she could've asked Xander what the main differences were between her old human form and her shifter one, she preferred to find out for herself.

When they reached her boss's office, she didn't bother knocking on the always closed door. She placed her hand in the middle of the probably fake wooden door and pushed with a little bit of force. To her satisfaction, the door ripped off the hinges with ease. She giggled as she watched the door stall upright for a split second, before it tilted forward and landed with a crash on the man's desk.

Instead of taking a step into the office, she stood at the doorway with her arms crossed over her chest. There was a perverse pleasure that she gained from the fear she spotted in his eyes. She smiled wider when his heart started to pound in his chest and his breathing increased to the point where she thought he might hyperventilate. Adding to his fear, she tipped her lips wider and gave him a vicious smile.

Sweetheart, are you trying to give the man a heart attack?

Nope, but he will have one when he sees you.

"Frost...what...what are you...doing here?"

"Expected me to be dead too, huh, Bob? Well, too bad for you, I guess."

His eyes widened and she thought he might wet himself as his eyes darted behind her to see Xander. He walked casually into the office, blocking out the light from the hallway beyond with his huge, muscular body. Bob's eyes didn't leave Xander. When Xander growled, a low vibration for a second, Bob swallowed visibly.

"Oh, Bob, how rude of me. This is Xander. He's my snow leopard-shifter mate. The one that you—yes, I know it was you, Bob—sent those mercenaries to kill."

Without waiting for a response, she sprinted forward, her movements unseen by Bob, until she appeared in front of him and lifted the fat fucker off the floor and pinned him to the wall behind his oversized desk.

Realizing how fun that had been, she turned and looked over her shoulder at Xander. Instead of meeting his gaze, her eyes wandered over his body. Today he wore a tight black tee that made his white hair and blue eyes stand out. The way he wore those pair of jeans should have been illegal. She wanted to pinch herself again when the swell of happiness bubbled in her chest at the thought of Xander being hers.

Sweetheart? Aren't you supposed to be scaring the living shit out of the man you have pinned to the wall? You can explore my body later.

Huh. *Promise?*

Xander laughed aloud, causing Bob to jerk in her grasp, but she didn't let go. She kept her eyes on Xander.

Promise.

"Well, then. Let's get this show on the road." She turned back to Bob and almost laughed when he squeaked in fear.

She learned that her thoughts, much like they did when she was human, pinged around in her head. But now, she could concentrate on one, the others falling silent in the background. She liked this shifter thing.

"Did you hire the mercenaries directly or were you paid to do it?"

"Go to hell."

To the surprise of both Xander and Bob, she released him. Ignoring their reactions, she paced in front of the gaudy desk, her hands tucked behind her back, every so often pinning Bob with her gaze.

"On one hand, I'm grateful that you sent me to the mountains as a tracker, because I was able to meet Xander. But on the other hand, I want to break your fucking neck for sending mercenaries to kill unsuspecting targets. Fortunately for me, the mercenaries were no match for the immortal assassins who were your targets, you stupid fucking idiot."

Bob, if possible, paled even more.

"You know you're in some serious shit, Bob, when you send flunkies with guns after trained…immortal…assassins."

The man didn't disappoint. He shook as fear enveloped him.

"Oh, you did know then, did you?" Her laugh should have turned his blood cold.

The sound cut off abruptly when she slammed the man back against the wall a little harder than necessary.

"You will give me every shred of information you have on those who hired you, or I will break every bone in your body, keeping you alive and awake the entire time."

Bob opened his mouth, his face pinched in anger. She knew that he wanted to get the last word in, he thrived on it, but the words died in his throat when Xander's growl filled the room and Bob clamped his mouth shut.

"Well?"

Bob refused to speak, so after waiting a half a minute, she curled her hand into a fist and bopped him on the nose. Not enough to crush his skull in, but enough to break his nose with a nice little snap. She allowed him to cry and fuss for a few minutes, calling her a few choice words, before she snapped it back into place with a twist of her fingers.

His nose stopped bleeding at her actions and she glared at him, deciding on a new strategy.

"You either tell me, or I'll give Xander a go at you. Remember— big, bad assassin, contracted by the government to kill people for a living."

Bob flinched when Xander took a step into the room. That was all it took for Bob to spill all of his secrets.

Fuck, am I not threatening enough?

No, sweetheart, you can scare the shit out of people with the best of them, but you should have broken his arm, not his nose.

I sense you're placating me.

She heard laughter in her head and she growled.

"Marcus. I was the middle man between Marcus and this mercenary group called Nightfall. I was paid a lot of money to get a tracker to lead them."

"What was the plan for Frost?" Xander asked, his voice low and deadly.

Bob visibly shook as he looked at Xander. "They could use her in any way they wanted, once they were finished with their mission. Then she was to be handed over to another man. I never got that man's name."

Xander lurched forward and lifted him by the collar of his shirt until he was face-to-face with an extremely pissed-off shifter. "And how much money did you take in order to sacrifice Frost's life?"

"A…quarter of a million dollars."

Xander tossed him aside with casual ease. Frost got a tiny bit of satisfaction when Bob hit the opposite wall harder than she had expected.

"Who would pay that much for a mission that would obviously fail?" Xander thought aloud.

"That would be me, Marcus." His voice floated in from the hallway. "I needed an advantage to lure you out, take you captive, and extract information from you."

Xander laughed, non-humorously, and it caused Marcus to clench his teeth together in frustration. The new addition looked a little like an evil henchmen in any 80s movie. His hair was military short; he wore all black with holsters strapped to his torso and a couple of knives sheathed against his thighs. Although it would have been a great look on Xander, except for the haircut, Marcus made it look ridiculous.

Marcus, distracted by his anger at Xander not taking him

seriously, left her free to search for a weapon that she could use if they needed to fight, having forgot, for a moment, about her newly acquired strength and speed. She dropped her head and cursed, but instead of ditching the weapon, she palmed it in her right hand and looked at Xander.

Her mate was completely relaxed. His stance was wide, with his arms crossed over his massive chest. She growled when she realized that Marcus had been perusing Xander's body for way too long, the evidence clearly outlined in the front area of his tight black pants.

"Oh, for fuck sake. He's my mate, you idiot. I know that you've been listening in on our conversation. We could scent you when we walked down the hallway."

What? Xander hadn't understood the first part of her outburst.

Marcus is attracted to you, and you could tell that if your gaze dropped down to his hard-on currently tenting the front of his pants.

I'll pass, thanks. Xander laughed before he pulled her in for a scorching kiss that left her throbbing and needy.

"Well, I guess that I have to kill you both now."

Before Marcus could raise the gun he unclipped when Xander kissed her, Frost threw the letter opener deep into his right shoulder and a millisecond later, stood in front of him. She ripped the gun out of his hand and reached for the letter opener. She turned the letter opener counterclockwise about a half an inch and drew a cry of absolute pain from the little fucker.

"That's for having me shot in the shoulder. That fucking hurt, you asshole."

She released her hold on the weapon protruding from Marcus, and he dropped straight to the ground, bleeding from his shoulder. She turned back to Bob.

"If you tell anyone anything we've said here today..." She shook her head and pierced him again with her gaze. "Well, I'll have Xander's friends pay you a visit. And trust me when I say this. You will feel every bit of pain they inflict on you before they decide to have mercy on you and kill you. Do you understand?"

Her growl was ferocious, promising plenty of pain, and Bob jerked backward enough to strike his head on the open filing cabinet behind him, effectively knocking himself out.

Xander pulled her back into his arms and kissed her until her knees felt weak. "That was the single hottest fucking thing I've ever seen in my life."

"I would like to go home now." Her growl was less than subtle.

"We could get naked and claim each other?"

Another kiss—this time she initiated it—but again, they were interrupted. A loud groan echoed throughout the room.

I don't think this man is in charge of anything.

You're right. But we'll have to call a meeting when we get home and see if the others know anything about Nightfall.

She paused for a moment before she met his gaze. *Do you really want to claim me?*

Yes, sweetheart. I've been waiting a lifetime for you.

A sense of rightness settled over her. His words made her heart beat faster and a smile tilted her lips up. Another, louder groan brought her out of her thoughts and she glanced down. "What should we do with them?"

"Fuck it." He laced their fingers together and led her out of the office. "Time to go home."

As she looked back, she knew that whoever hired Bob and Marcus wouldn't give up just because she and Xander had found a link between the mercenaries and those who hired them. Whoever hired these two inept men would have a plan for a long game, but for the life of her, she had no idea how she fit into the overall plan.

Chapter Five

Xander

Xander managed to unlock the door before they burst through, their lips devouring each other, as he struggled with shutting and locking the door after they passed through. As elegant as ever, Xander tripped and managed to land on his back with Frost sprawled on top of him, his arms wrapped tightly around her to keep her safe. He glanced at her shocked face and couldn't hold back the bark of laughter that escaped his throat.

She blinked before she glanced down at his lips and pressed her body closer to his. "At least we're already on a flat surface." Her smile was dazzling.

The fingers of his right hand brushed through her long, dark hair, while the other pressed against her lower back, bringing her even closer to his body. He was about to capture her lips in a scorching kiss that would definitely lead to more, but they were interrupted by a loud cough coming from the living room.

Frost raised her gaze and glanced into the living room. She squeaked indelicately as she scrambled off his lap, but he wanted to keep her close and whoever was in the house could fuck off. He growled when she managed to stand; when he reached for her, she sidestepped him, still staring toward the living room. He watched her eyes widen and a flush stain her cheeks, so he tipped his head back while still laying on the floor and he spotted everyone. And he meant everyone. *Fuck.*

He reluctantly got to his feet before he reached for Frost's hand and interlaced their fingers together, giving her a little squeeze of reassurance.

Liv, of course, not caring about the awkwardness in the room, darted forward and enveloped Frost in a hug. Xander smiled when he saw that Frost hadn't hesitated to wrap her arms around the smaller woman in return.

"How did your first shift go?" Liv asked.

"I haven't…shifted. It's been three days since I woke up and nothing. I remember the transition, well-developed bits and pieces, but I woke up feeling strong and healthy, but no shift."

"Then…well, where have you guys been?"

"Oh, yeah. We just arrived back from Denver. We went to confront my boss, who about peed his pants when Xander walked into his office." She laughed and the others smiled.

"I should probably start from the beginning. My boss, Bob, had hired me out to the mercenaries as a tracker to find the immortals, although I didn't know at the time he meant everyone here. We thought he would give us the name of the person who hired him. At first, he wasn't cooperative, even though I thought my threat to break all of his bones one by one was pretty scary. He didn't unfortunately. Am I not that scary?" Frost asked.

"No," Kane stated.

"Not at all," Seth piped up.

"About as much as Liv." Kai received a glare from his wife and he wiped the smile off his face.

"Anyway…we found out that a group called Nightfall hired the mercenaries. Marcus, a human mercenary, acted as the go-between, and contracted the mercenaries to kill, well, you guys. At least I got to stab Marcus." Frost beamed at that.

"Why did you stab him?" It was Ax this time.

"He was eye-fucking Xander. Rude, right?"

The chorus of laughter brought Frost's gaze from Liv's and she took in the rest of the assassins in the room. When she spotted Gunnar she nodded, and Kane she smiled, but when she spotted Seth, her smile grew wider.

"Hey, kid. I told you I'd be okay."

Seth stepped forward, hand-in-hand with his beautiful dark auburn-haired wife, and side-hugged Frost. She hugged him back.

"This is my mate and wife, Aubrey."

Of course, Frost hugged her. "It's nice to meet you. You have a very sweet man."

Aubrey smiled and returned the hug and Frost relaxed. Xander took her hand in his and introduced her to Hunter, Thomas, Isaac, and then Ghost. Frost's eyes widened as she glanced at Ghost's hair, very similar to his. As she was introduced, she either hugged them or shook their hand, but she turned around and ran into Axel. She paused; her gaze slowly traveled higher until she reached Ax's smiling face.

"Hey, honey. I'm Axel."

Xander rolled his eyes. *The man didn't know when to quit.*

"Sure you are. Not a chance, honey, not a chance." Frost patted his chest and stepped around him, moving to Xander's side.

At that moment, Jade came out of the kitchen, a little hesitant. Frost pulled away from Xander and walked toward her, carefully, as if she were afraid Jade would strike out at her. Xander stood still, knowing Frost wanted to apologize, but he could only hope that Jade was as forgiving as he thought she would be.

Without a word, Frost pulled Jade in for a long hug. Xander relaxed when Jade returned the hug. They stood there for long minutes before Frost pulled back.

"I'm sorry, so sorry, for how I acted when I first saw you."

"It happens…a lot."

Frost flinched at that, but continued. "Just because I was in pain was no excuse for taking it out on you. I am sorry. I would like to try to be friends with you."

Jade smiled at her. "I would like that. Are you hungry?" Without waiting for a response, Jade pulled Frost into the kitchen. "So, who was undressing Xander with their gaze?"

All the shifters flooded into the kitchen. Xander made a plate after making sure Frost had a plate for herself and sat down next to his mate as she explained about Marcus and what they encountered in Denver.

"He was threatening to kill us, but he couldn't pull his gaze away from Xander long enough to back up his threat. I mean, it's fine to look, but when his attraction became evident, I figured it was time to drive a letter opener through his shoulder."

"Nightfall, huh?" Ghost asked.

Xander turned to look at his boss. He knew something that they didn't.

"They are a shifters-only company that has been trying for years to take over our contract with the government, without success." Ghost took a bite, but his brow was furrowed in concern.

"Why only shifters?" Frost asked.

Ghost cleared his throat, clearly uncomfortable. "They see vampires and humans as lower life-forms and believe they shouldn't exist."

They all grew quiet. Ghost turned to stare at Frost, and Xander groaned and cursed under his breath when he realized where Ghost's thoughts had led him.

"Why didn't they turn Frost if they suspected she was part shifter?"

Liv, of course, had already thought about it. "I don't think flooding a human, even a half-shifter, with venom when they are a destined mate of another would work. Most likely it will kill the human. I think the only reason that you guys didn't die from the venom in the first place was that one, you were stronger than most humans who had been bitten, and secondly, I think that you were turned because your mates hadn't been born at the time you transitioned."

"So they understood that I was part shifter and their plan was to meet Xander and have me transition, and then, what, recruit us both?"

"I wouldn't put it past them. They believe that all shifters should stick together. They sensed Frost was a half-shifter somehow and knew that she wouldn't transition until she found her mate. So, they must know something that we don't, and took a chance orchestrating the meet using the human mercenaries as bait. And since we are the only immortals in the area, they figured that they would have a good chance in finding Frost's mate among us."

"They must not know anything about Dark Company if they thought anyone here would abandon their family because they expected shifters to stick together." Seth sounded disgusted.

"We are untraceable. Xander made sure to cover all our tracks including money, property, and even identities. We only have one government contact and it would be next to impossible for anyone to find out about them. Trust me, we've tried but they are untraceable. Hell, we aren't even paid by traditional means."

Xander shook his head. He hated the thought of having an all-out battle with another group of immortals. But if they threatened his family, he and the others would take care of them without hesitation or regret. "I'll start a search for the hierarchy. What are we going to do about them once I find them?"

"We'll make that decision when we're better informed."

Frost turned to Liv. "Am I a full shifter?"

"We don't really know. You have all the attributes of a shifter—regenerative healing, strength, speed, and the transition you went through mirrored Ara's—but we aren't sure why you haven't shifted yet."

Frost blinked in surprise when a tall, dark-haired shifter walked in with a beautiful woman. She had long, cascading dark hair and the lightest brown eyes she'd ever seen.

"Are you guys talking about me?"

Xander stood and reached his hand out for Frost, smiling at her when she linked their fingers together. "Hey, Ara. This is my mate, Frost. Frost, this is Ara."

Ara's smile was dazzling as she beamed at him and threw herself in his arms. "You found her! I told you you would." Ara pulled back and still smiling, hugged Frost tightly. "And she's gorgeous."

"I know. I should have listened to you."

Ara placed her mouth close to Frost's ear, but he overheard anyway. "Take care of him."

"I will," Frost promised as she beamed at her new friend.

Ara turned. "And this is my mate, Reaper."

Frost shook his hand, but her eyes widened in excitement. "That is a wicked name."

Reaper laughed. He took everyone by surprise when he pulled

Frost closer and hugged her. She smiled at him, but stepped back into Xander's arms and reached for his hand.

I like them, all of them.

They like you, too, sweetheart. I knew they would.

"How did it go?" Ghost asked the newcomers.

Ara frowned. "He was already dead, and it was very sloppy work. His throat was ripped out and we could smell a shifter, maybe two."

Ghost filled them in on what he and Frost had discovered, and they agreed that more research was necessary before they acted. Xander would do the computer search, hacking into systems for any information available on Nightfall. Ghost would check in with his contact. Jade and Gunnar would go to the latest location and track the scent of those responsible.

By the time everyone headed out, both he and Frost were exhausted. After he made sure that the house was locked and the alarm set, he scooped Frost into his arms and started up the stairs.

"I can walk, you know?"

"Not when I have a chance to hold you. I will always choose to be near you."

"Holding my hand isn't enough?" Frost smiled.

"Nope."

They readied for bed before they settled into bed, lying side by side. He kissed her nose, one cheek, and then the other, before he reached her lips. Lazily, they kissed, never deepening the kiss, just enjoying the simple touch. When her eyes drooped from tiredness, he tucked her against his chest and smiled as he held her. Although their plans were changed when they came home, he was happy that Frost had met his entire family. He had no doubt that they would love her, but he had been nervous for her. And it all had gone perfectly.

"I'm going to get to see you naked again sometime soon, right?"

He chuckled and pulled her closer. "Yes. And don't worry, we have all the time in the world, sweetheart."

She huffed her dissatisfaction, but brushed a kiss to his chest and snuggled closer. Soon, her breathing evened out and Xander couldn't wipe the smile from his face. *His mate. He'd finally found his mate.*

Chapter Six

Frost

Frost felt the warmth of Xander pressed against her back as his soft breaths brushed against the back of her neck. His chest moved with each breath and she smiled that she'd woken up in his arms every morning since she transitioned. Sleeping in Xander's arms was new to her, but she found that she liked it. She fell asleep faster and slept better as he cradled her close every night.

She had stopped suppressing the smile that would form on her lips whenever she thought about how happy she was each time Xander held her hand or pulled her onto his lap to keep her close. But the mornings were the best.

Over the past week, she realized that she hadn't needed a lot of sleep as a shifter mix, as she had started referring to herself. She had watched as Xander worked his magic, tracking down the boss of the company, Nightfall. He had named himself Anzû, and according to mythology, he was the Akkadian demon who stole the Tablet of Destinies in order to make himself the highest god in the land. Frost had rolled her eyes when Xander had told her what he'd found. *What an ass.*

While Xander had been busy with the search for Anzû and the uncovering of his organization, Frost had gotten to know the rest of the assassins better. She spent a lot of time with Jade, now that she'd been forgiven for how Frost acted when they first met. It was nice to be part of such a large, eclectic group where she could be herself without people thinking that she was either crazy or blunt.

And because of what Xander had been working on, he had yet to fulfill his promise that she could explore his naked body. She didn't want to get in the way of his work, but this morning she had woken with a throbbing between her legs and when his arm tightened around her, she ground her bottom against his hard cock.

Frost knew that Xander was a heavy sleeper, especially early in the morning. Although Xander always slept naked, she hadn't been ready for that next step and still slept in her tee and panties. But she now found them stifling and she couldn't wait for him to remove them.

She turned in his arms and with slightly shaky fingers, she traced the tattoo on his left shoulder. She could feel the slight raise in his skin where the black ink had been marked on his flawless skin, but she loved the intricate detail and spent the next few minutes memorizing the feel and the look of it. She moved to trace another tattoo over his right pectoral. She had never been brave enough to get a tattoo, although she had been fascinated by some of the designs that she'd seen. On Xander, it looked sexy and added depth to his smooth olive skin.

Without waiting another second, she slowly lowered the sheet that covered his waist and couldn't help but stare at every inch of skin she exposed to her view. She longed to reach out and touch him there, but she didn't want to wake him before she looked her fill. She felt naughty, taking advantage of him while he slept, but she was hoping to make him lose control and he would finally make love to her and she could be his, completely.

Every inch of Xander appealed to her. From the tilt of his lips when she said or did something he found amusing, to how his ice-blue eyes sparked with emotion whenever she asked him to kiss her. And his body—his rock hard, sexy-as-sin body—made her core clench and her body heat with need each time she woke next to him. She couldn't help it. But the way he said her name right before he kissed her, devoured her mouth, had her shivering in his arms.

Not wanting to waste one more second without knowing this man, her mate, intimately, she eased herself out of his hold and glanced back to see whether she had woken him. His eyes were closed and his chest moved up and down with steady breaths, so she flipped onto her hands and knees and crawled toward him.

For a few minutes, she wondered where she should start. Each time she would touch him, she got a thrill that would have her craving more. Now was her chance and she wasn't going to waste it.

Burrowing her face against his neck, she inhaled. His scent alone had her closing her eyes and biting her lip to prevent a moan from escaping. When she felt a little more under control, she pressed a kiss to the soft skin under his ear, hearing his breathing stagger for a moment before resuming the regular rhythm. She moved down to his collarbone, kissing across it until she reached the dip between the two, running her tongue up the indentation and licking until she reached his chin. She froze when he placed one hand on the small of her back to keep her close and she waited until he relaxed back into sleep before she continued.

With her body practically vibrating, she placed small kisses on his chest, moving her touch back and forth, tasting his skin every once in a while with a small dart of her tongue. She moved to prevent her moan from escaping her throat, and when she reached his nipples, she swirled her tongue around one nub, loving how responsive he was. When she pulled back and blew on the wet area, she watched as his skin darkened as the nub pulled taut.

She hadn't realized that he'd woken until his hand spanned over her waist and squeezed; his hands tightened as she took the other in her mouth and sucked.

The next time she looked up, his gaze swirled with the haze of sleep and a definite glint of desire for her. She continued to move down his body, tasting and nipping as she went. She loved that she could kiss every rise and fall throughout his body, every indent of muscle, and the cut of his hips that led to his straining cock that pressed up against her stomach.

She straddled his lower legs and without hesitation, she bent forward and licked the head of his cock. A drop rolled onto her tongue and she tasted him before she swallowed the entire head into her mouth. Her tongue swirled around the slit to taste more of him. At the same time, she stored every grunt and moan she drew from him, learning the feel of him and what gave him pleasure. When his breath would catch in his throat, she repeated the movement, loving his reactions to her.

By the time she had moved on from taking just the head of his cock in her mouth, they were both panting, but she didn't stop. Torturing both of them, she took as much of him as she could, feeling the head of his cock pressed against the back of her throat, and by instinct alone, swallowed.

In the time it took her to blink, she found herself flat on her back, staring at Xander, who kept his arms straight, holding himself away from her. Not wanting to lose the momentum she built, she wrapped her arms around his shoulders and pulled him closer for a searing kiss. They both moaned, the sounds captured in the other's mouth, but she needed something more. She found her hips lifting off the bed of their own accord, looking for the friction she so desperately needed.

He pulled back from the kiss, his lips swollen and his pupils so dilated that she could barely see the ice-blue she had loved from the moment he turned his eyes toward her.

"Why...did you stop...me?" She found herself panting as she asked the question.

"I didn't want to finish before we have even started, sweetheart."

"So…we can finally make love?"

He pressed a light kiss to her lips. "I would like nothing more than to make love to you."

"Well, it's about time. I've done everything but hold up a sign that read 'make love to me, now' on it."

Xander smiled and brushed the hair from her forehead, having her breath catch in her throat. "I understood the hints, but you're new to this life and being a mate. I wanted you to be sure, since for me, this is forever."

"I feel the same way, Xander." She felt her heart squeeze and tears spring to her eyes as she told him the truth.

He truly kissed her then, but he refused to lower his entire weight on top of her. He savored her mouth as she wiggled under him. When she lay there panting and moaning, he pulled back.

"I need you."

At his words, she felt her core flood and her body heat with need. "Yes."

He removed the gray tank that she'd slept in, but when his hand trailed down her damaged side, he paused. His eyes were glued to her pink lace panties, the ones she'd bought during their trip to Denver for the purpose of tempting him. When he glanced up and met her eyes, the hunger that was etched on his face had her blow out the breath she didn't realize she'd been holding. She moaned when he trailed a finger along the thin waistband, barely touching her, as he watched the skin under his touch quiver.

His desperate gaze jerked back to hers, and without hesitation, she nodded.

Moving with excruciating slowness, he lowered her panties over her flared hips before he slid his fingers down her inner thighs, until he discarded the slip of material somewhere behind his head.

She held her breath, waiting to see what he would do next. As his gaze roamed over her body, not missing an inch of what she thought was an overly curvy one, she felt as though she was being caressed from his gaze alone. Her skin felt heated, not anything like when she transitioned; instead, it felt as though his hot gaze brought every one of her nerve endings to life.

Her eyes closed as she savored the sensations of his gaze. The rustle of sheets had her groan as he moved away from her, but soon his warm hands were gently pushing apart her thighs. Her eyes popped open when he settled between her legs and his wide shoulders opened her up to his view. Instead of feeling self-conscious as she normally would, she found that Xander's actions had her panting with need.

His gaze met hers. "Is it okay if I taste you?"

Her strangled moan sounded as close to a yes as she could communicate. When he flattened his tongue near her leaking entrance and licked a swath up her heated lips toward her bundle of nerves, her thoughts unraveled and she couldn't speak coherently if she tried.

He feasted on her—there was no other word for it—as she gasped and thrashed against the mattress, fisting the sheets as she tried to ground herself to reality. Her words, the ones that she could push past her clogged throat sounded contradictory as she tried to convey that it was too much and not enough at the same time.

"You taste as sweet as I thought you would." His voice rumbled over her.

She had to bite her lip, preventing a dirty moan that wanted to escape her throat. But she couldn't concentrate on his voice or his words while the sensations of pleasure she'd never experienced before washed over her. She dropped her head back against the pillow and savored each lick as he went back to tasting her.

Unconsciously, she threaded her fingers through his soft hair and tried not to close her hand into a fist. But when he slid one long finger inside her, she clamped down on him and tightened her grip on his hair. The overwhelming sensations of his tongue, his finger, even his breaths against her heated skin had her chanting his name.

He swirled his tongue around her bud, the first finger then joined by another, adding to the throbbing when he moved both in and out of her with practiced ease. It all had her teetering on the edge. With one last suck on her clit along with the crook of his fingers deep inside her, she shouted her release before she moaned his name in a way that she had tried to prevent earlier. Her body arched off the bed, all her muscles locked down as he drew out her orgasm.

Before she could take a breath, her eyelids fluttered closed and the sounds around her ceased.

Chapter Seven

Xander

Xander sensed more than spotted when Frost lost consciousness, and immediately crawled up to lay by her side. He cradled her head on his chest and blew out a relieved sigh when he felt her hot, staggered breaths brush over his sensitized skin. But his cock, at that most inopportune moment, jumped as Frost moved against him, her skin warm and her scent calling to him like nothing ever had.

When he woke earlier, he could've sworn he was dreaming as he watched Frost kiss down his neck, and then his chest, taking one of his nipples into her sweet mouth. He shook off the last remnants of sleep and his eyes widened comically as he watched her kiss down his body. Her soft hair brushed a trail of heat against his skin that had him jump against her stomach.

He hadn't wanted to pressure her by moving their relationship into an area that she might not be comfortable with, and tried to keep his hands to himself, but his Frost was pure temptation. With every brush of her lips and the touch of her hand on his skin, and he wanted to carry her upstairs and love her until they were too sore to move. It was as close to torture as he'd ever experienced. But when she paused at his hips and her blue-green eyes flashed at him, he realized how much he'd been craving her touch.

Soon, the trail her mouth had taken had pushed him straight to the edge. It was pure heaven when she wrapped her mouth around his cock, and he found it sexy as hell that she had taken him deep in her mouth without any hesitation. But he would embarrass himself before they even started if she continued.

When she landed gently on the bed, he knew that he needed to taste her and the desire roared through his veins. It was sexy as hell that she trusted him as he settled between her thighs. Her reactions to his touch pushed him to explore her further, until the rush of her orgasm had her pass out from the pleasure.

Pulled from his thoughts when she moaned against his chest, he pulled back and couldn't help the concern he felt for her. She had been out for a good five minutes, and all he used was his tongue and lips. And, okay, his fingers, too. But there was a smile of satisfaction on her face as she opened her hand on his chest and roamed every inch of skin she could touch. Soon, touching wasn't enough, and she crawled on his lap.

When her wetness brushed against his cock, he stifled a moan and threw his head back on the pillow. Nothing had ever felt so good in his life.

"I want to hear you, Xander. I want to know that *I'm* making you scream with pleasure."

She lifted herself off him before she pressed her hips forward, brushing her lips against his cock and covering him with her wetness that he'd tasted only minutes before. She sat back, placing herself farther out of his reach, and he fisted his hands by his side so he couldn't reach for her and pull her on top of him.

He let out a choked sob when she reached for the base of his cock and squeezed. A moan tore out of him when she used her come to easily slide her hand up and down his length, using the perfect amount of pressure in order to drive him out of his mind.

"Please, sweetheart. I need—"

With quick, sure movements, she raised herself on her knees and before he could finish his plea, she sank down onto his cock. He flinched slightly when he could feel her muscles as they clamped down on the head of his cock. It was too tight, too warm, too pleasurable, too everything. And he groaned when he realized it was only the beginning. He thought that he would hurt her if he made any movements, so he held his hips still and allowed her to set her own pace and take her own pleasure.

"Touch me, Xander."

His hands clamped around her hips, loving the soft skin underneath the rough skin of his fingers and palms, and she moaned when he squeezed. He couldn't help but run one hand up the soft skin of her stomach, until they were close to her beautifully rounded breasts. Using his forefinger and thumb, he added a slight pressure to her nipple and was rewarded with a low and dirty moan.

She sank down slowly onto his cock, never showing any signs of discomfort.   He hadn't realized that curses left his lips until she paused and smiled down at him.

"I'm trying to fuck you."

She bent down and kissed him.   The movement pressed him deeper inside her as she moved closer, and he felt surrounded by her tight, warm heat.   He breathed deep, loving her scent that surrounded him.

"Xander," she breathed.

His name on her lips had a groan emerging from his throat and he darted up to thread his fingers through her hair as he captured her lips in a searing kiss.   He loved when she moaned into his mouth and wrapped her arms around his shoulders.   Her hips drove forward, small movements that sent tremors of bliss throughout his body, as she searched for friction.

He released her lips and lay back down.   His thumb reached toward her clit and rubbed circles around the sensitive area, until she clamped down on him and moaned.

"Take what you want from me, sweetheart."

She lifted her hips a fraction, hissing at the sensations, before driving back down onto him.   She tried a couple more times, but she shivered as the sensations overwhelmed her.   Her chest was flushed, along with her beautiful face.   "I don't know how."

"You've…never, before?"

She shook her head, her hands pressed against his chest as she squeezed him.

"I never found myself attracted to anyone, until you, so I didn't care to gain any knowledge with someone else. Remember, I'm awkward around people."

He kissed her hard and flipped her onto her back, never removing himself from deep inside her. He deepened the kiss, and shivered as he drew another moan from her. His chest swelled with pride whenever she reacted to his touch. When they broke the kiss, she gasped for breath as he buried his face into her neck, loving her scent and the salty taste as he pressed his lips to her skin.

"Show me."

The small plea made his heart ache and at that moment, he wanted her to remember every touch, caress, and pleasurable sensation that he could give her. With one hand on her hip and the other pressed against the pillow near her head, he pulled back until the head of his cock was seated just inside her and angled her hips before he thrust deep inside.

"Oh, oh. More, please. Xander. More."

He moved his hips forward, changing the angle and the speed of his thrusts, finding what Frost needed from him. Each stroke set her afire, her moans almost unraveling him and soon, her movements matched his. She thrust her hips up to meet his, driving him even deeper inside her. She squeezed him each time he moved back, as if she wanted to keep him inside her for as long as possible. With her hands roaming over his chest and back, a growl rumbled through him and continued as she cupped his ass and drove him harder against her.

He moved his mouth down her neck, lightly biting her collarbone, but staving off the need to claim her. He needed time to fully explain what claiming meant to him, and what it would mean for her. She moaned and angled her neck toward him, but he continued his exploration until he reached one of her pebbled nipples and drew it into his mouth. He swirled his tongue around her several times, savoring her taste, before sucking the bud deep in his mouth and moaned against her skin. Soon, he moved to the other, not wanting to neglect any part of her body that would add to her pleasure.

Sensations melded together, overwhelming both of them, and soon he could feel the tingle in his spine that signaled his impending release. But he wanted her pleasure first, so he reached down and rubbed his thumb along her clit.

She moaned and gripped his shoulders, anchoring herself to him as she moaned his name.

He forced open his eyes, wanting to see her flushed skin and her reactions this close to their orgasms, but it took him by surprise when her skin, all over her body, glowed.

He increased his thrusts, feeling close to the edge and slowly losing control. When she blinked up at him, she gasped as she caught the glow on her forearm, her hands gripping Xander tightly.

"What?" She met his gaze.

But before he could answer her, even if he could explain it to himself, pleasure surged through his entire body as she clenched down on his cock. He felt the flood of her wet heat as it covered his cock and he lost all control. With her name on his lips, repeating it over and over again, he drove in once, and then again, before he pressed himself deep inside and released. A roar ripped through his throat and his cock continued to pulse for long minutes.

When he could focus past his pleasure, he pulled her close and noticed that the glow that had been so prominent before was now slowly fading. He pressed kisses on her forehead, cheeks, and lips as he stroked her hip as they came down from their high. She shivered as their bodies slowly cooled, and he rolled to his side and gathered her close before he reached for the comforter, pulling it over them, and smiled against her hair when she snuggled closer.

"You're mine now, sweetheart. I won't ever be able to let you go."

She kissed his chest. "I don't want to be apart from you. I'm so glad that you found me."

Xander kissed her gently, unable to stay away from her.

"When did I stop glowing?"

"Not too long ago. We should sleep for a few more hours, before Ghost orders us back to our search. He wants me to find the money trail between Nightfall and the government."

She nodded, and her soft hair brushed against his hot skin. He squeezed her, enjoying her being in his arms, and before long, he heard her breathing slow as she settled into sleep.

His arm tightened when he realized how happy she made him. She had told him that she felt the same way, and she wasn't afraid to express it. He felt guilty for not claiming her. He wanted her to make the decision on her future with all the details he could provide. Although he loved that she dove into everything with abandon, forever was a long time and she needed to make an informed decision, or he would always feel as if he pushed her into being his mate.

And soon, he would explain everything, before he would find those who truly threatened her and his family, and he would destroy them.

With one last press of his lips to her forehead, he closed his eyes and listened to her breathing until he was pulled into sleep.

Chapter Eight

Frost

Frost woke up and without looking at the clock, stumbled in the darkness toward the bathroom as the fullness of her bladder made itself known. She caught sight of the clock on the nightstand as she closed the door behind her and groaned at the time—three a.m. She had woken just two hours before, and two hours before that, having to pee each time.

They had to be up in a few hours to investigate the lead that Xander had found between Nightfall and the mercenaries. They were having the others over for breakfast before the sun rose so the vampires could be there.

She tried to clear her head enough to think about why she had been getting out of bed so often, and other than a stupid infection that she hoped she couldn't get now that she was a shifter mix, but nothing suggested itself to her. All she knew was that she usually slept like the dead, but after waking up so often, she felt groggy and her mind slow. She loved sleep, even though she didn't need as many hours as a shifter mix, but when she lay in Xander's arms, she never wanted to leave the bed. Now, the more she thought about it, the more irritated she grew. She would ask Liv about it later when she saw her for the meeting.

She flipped on the light, not willing to take the risk of falling if she blinked too slowly or, heaven forbid, she nodded off to sleep while sitting up. She squinted as she made her way across the room, and only stubbed her toe once on the side of the cabinet and managed not to curse aloud. As she finished, she felt a bit more awake. Her mind flashed back to the moment she noticed that her skin had glowed, right before her orgasm struck and left her breathless and shaking. The first time they'd made love. Each time they had loved—and if she were honest with herself, it had been every few hours when they were awake and a couple of times during the night—every day since the first time, her skin hadn't glowed, even though her feelings for Xander grew more intense. She thought, like the rest of her that was different than everybody else, that it was an anomaly that wasn't anything to worry about and she brushed it off.

Grateful that she could head back to bed, she glanced up and noticed the circles under her eyes and shook her head. She wondered whether she would even wake up before the other's arrived. She washed her hands and splashed water on her face, feeling the cool calming her, before she reached for a towel and dried her hands and face. Pulling the towel away, she blinked her eyes at the harsh light from the bathroom and caught a glimpse of her stomach. Her eyes widened, before she blinked again, and still her brain was slow to understand.

Although she hadn't noticed it a few minutes before, there was a definite roundness to her stomach. It now hung a little past her waistline. She felt surprisingly calm when she lifted her shirt and tucked it underneath her breasts to expose her stomach completely. Her hands opened over her belly and she closed her eyes, straining to listen. Waiting several minutes, she learned the sound and the rhythm of her own heartbeat before she tried to find another that would be softer, quieter.

There. The faint beat of another heart, muffled, almost indistinguishable.

The realization woke her faster than anything else could have. She bit her lip to hold back a gasp that wanted to escape and she listened to the tiny heartbeat in her womb. She was mesmerized for several minutes as pure joy surged through her. But her joy faltered as she thought about her mate, sleeping on the other side of the door in the bedroom.

Would he be happy?

Angry?

Would it be the end of their relationship?

For the past few weeks, she'd known that she loved Xander, but during the same time, he'd never indicated that he felt the same way about her. Sure, he cared for her, treated her as though she was the most important person in his life, but he hadn't claimed her. Each time his teeth scraped against her skin, she would hold her breath and hope that he would do exactly as she wanted, but he pulled away as if the thought stopped him cold.

She wondered how being pregnant was even possible. She knew that Liv, Ara, and Aubrey couldn't conceive because, according to Liv, they were in a form of stasis after their transition. Although blood still pumped in their veins, it was for the purpose of keeping them alive, not to procreate. And she had gone through the transition, having the exact same aches and pains as Ara had described hers to be. But the one main difference was that Ara shifted after she came out of it; Frost hadn't. It never really bothered her that she couldn't, because she had the other attributes of being a shifter and had been ecstatic with her new mate to care very much.

What if I'm not his true mate? That could be a reason for him not to claim me.

He doesn't want me, does he?

With those confusing thoughts swirling around her brain, she sat down on the floor near the tub and rubbed her belly.

Her body sagged and for a few desperate minutes, she welcomed the feeling of numbness as it washed over her, leaving her thoughts surprisingly quiet as she processed the pain. But then her practical side kicked in and realized that she would have to figure out what to do. Despite her own feelings, all that mattered now was her son.

Xander might not want her, but he would want his child, and she would never deny him access to his son. Just because he didn't want her didn't mean that he wouldn't want their son. She would never accept anything less than love. Xander would try to be noble about it, force himself to do the right thing because he was old-fashioned like that, but time with their son would be different than time with her. She would accept it, no matter how much her heart might be broken.

But right now, she would have to learn all about her pregnancy and how to protect her son, and she knew the one place she could go. She knew that they would support her, but Frost wouldn't come between his family and Xander. So, she decided that she would go to Liv for advice and then from there, she would figure it out.

Pushing herself off the floor, she walked toward the door and flipped the light off. She quietly dressed and headed downstairs. She found her coat near the door and wrapped it tightly around her body. With numb fingers, she unarmed the security system before rearming it and stepping outside into the cold January morning, locking the door behind her.

Silently, she made her way toward the copse of trees, making sure she was far enough away from Xander's house, before she started to run full speed toward her destination.

Barely out of breath after the seven-mile run, she reached the perimeter of the property and hesitated, knowing that anyone in the house would be alerted once she tripped the alarm. Although she didn't want a crowd around when she explained that she was pregnant, and silently thought about the fact her mate didn't want her, she took a deep breath and walked toward the front door.

The flood lights illuminated her clearly from the driveway. She could already see Kai standing on the porch by the front door and her steps faltered. Kai ran forward and pulled her into a hug. She let the tears that she'd been holding back flow.

Kai opened his mouth, but quickly snapped his teeth closed when she knew he detected the same small heartbeat that she had minutes early. Without hesitation, he lifted her in his arms and carried her into the house. Liv was waiting inside.

Liv appeared in front of her the moment the door closed behind Kai, and she took Frost from Kai's arms and gently set her on the couch.

"How far along, sweetie?"

Frost felt a pang of hurt, but pushed it down and smiled at Liv. Of course, Kai would communicate with Liv the moment he learned about her condition. Her smile faltered seconds later when she remembered that she wouldn't have anything close to the love they shared. Instead of wallowing, she concentrated on the question Liv posed.

"Two weeks. When we made love for the first time, my skin glowed. It was the first and only time it had happened. I'm guessing I conceived then."

Liv was so familiar with her that she placed her hand over Frost's stomach without asking. She felt a sense of calm as it washed over her from Liv's touch, and she felt as though she could breathe for the first time since she spotted the bump.

"Where's Xander?"

"I discovered the little bump on my millionth trip to the bathroom tonight." She rolled her eyes, she couldn't help it. "I didn't want to disturb him because he'd been sleeping so soundly."

Liv softened her gaze, sensing there was more to it and Frost cracked. "I don't know if he wants me. He hasn't claimed me, despite ample opportunities to do so, and he hasn't told me how he feels. He keeps reminding me that we're mates, but I haven't shifted, so why would he want a defective mate in the first place?"

"Are you going to keep the baby from him?"

Frost gasped and shook her head until she felt a bit dizzy. "No, he's the father. I would never do that. Even if he doesn't want me, he'll want him." She choked on the last word and rubbed gentle circles on her belly.

Liv nodded, satisfied. "Although it's been two weeks, he seems bigger than a normal baby, almost like he's months old instead of weeks. May I lift your shirt?"

Frost nodded. But before Liv could move her shirt out of the way, the front door crashed against the wall and she flinched at the sound. Xander stomped through the entrance into the living room where they were sitting and stood in front of her. His eyes were both full of fear and anger, the anger currently winning over the other.

She lowered her head onto her hand and rubbed at her brow, groaning aloud. *Fuck.* She then remembered her promise not to leave Xander again.

Steeling herself, she glanced up and prepared herself for whatever he wanted to say to her. The anger that radiated from him had her moving her hands to the front of her belly, holding her little man protectively.

Xander paused and closed his mouth. His eyes followed her hands as they rubbed against her stomach. She watched as his eyes widened as he spotted the baby bump for the first time since he walked in. When he blew out a breath and ran a hand through his hair, all the anger and fear that marred his face when he arrived disappeared in an instant.

"Are you pregnant?"

She gritted her teeth as a pain that she didn't know she could ever feel and still be alive ripped through her chest. He sounded less than happy at his realization and she braced herself for the actual rejection that was coming. "Yes."

It completely shocked her when he dropped straight to his knees in front of her and wrapped his arms around her. He buried his head against her chest. He squeezed her close to him, but she had no idea what this meant.

She sensed more than heard Kai and Liv exit the room, but she continued to sit there on the couch. She was stunned by Xander's reaction and as she tried to figure out what it meant, her mind kept blanking on the possibilities. Warmed by the embrace, she wanted to lean into him and hold him, but she held herself stiffly, prepared for anything he might say, whether hurtful or not.

After a long while, Xander raised his head and captured her lips in a kiss that wasn't rushed, but instead was sweet and loving.

"I'm sorry, I'm so sorry." His ragged voice reached her ears and she found herself sinking into his arms. His hold tightened as he continued. "I've always been cautious, it's my nature, but I should have told you how I felt from the moment I brought you home."

"How…" Her voice broke and she had to start again. "How do you feel?"

"I love you. I will always love you, for the rest of my existence. I wanted to claim you so many times, but my practical side kicked in and I knew I had to talk to you about what it meant, and it scared me to think that the knowledge would drive you away. But I did that with my stupidity. When I claim you, you will always carry my mark on you, and I want you to claim me as well. It means that I will kill for you, sacrifice my life for you. As long as you're happy and whole, I will be happy, because you are my life now."

His eyes were pleading as he looked at her, and she shook herself out of her stupor.

"I love you, too, Xander. I felt it the moment you came into my life."

For a long time, they held each other's gazes as he caressed her face. He kissed her and when he pulled back, he glanced down, but not before she spotted the sheer happiness on his face at the thought of a baby.

"Can I…touch…"

She grunted her displeasure at him asking in the first place and grabbed his wrists, yanking up her shirt with one hand and moving his opened hands over her belly.

Xander's face lit up and she knew that he'd felt the same

connection to their little man when he touched her. She could feel the vibration in her belly, a little bit like a burst of happiness, before it settled down into a hum.

"You've given me more than I could have ever expected. The moment you came into my life, you gave me a sense of peace I've never known, and a love that I could hardly believe I could find. But more than our connection, we share our baby. I promise, I will never hold anything back from you again."

"I know." Frost smiled and leaned forward to kiss him, a small touch of reassurance. "Are you going to claim me now?"

"Yes. That means our connection will be unbreakable."

"But I'm…I haven't shifted yet. What if I'm damaged in some way?"

"Every immortal is different. There is no normal. None of the immortals remember their transitions or much about the first few weeks after. You can't compare shifters to other shifters, much less shifters to vampires. Take Ara. She's brilliant with her telekinesis, which grew stronger after she transitioned, but it takes her close to twenty minutes to shift completely. Liv would rather heal than hurt, and each time Kai or the others go out on assignment, she's a wreck. Aubrey had been a vampire of ten years before she met Seth and knew nothing about other immortals until she met us.

"You are who you are, sweetheart. Whether you shift or not, I'm in love with you and from now on, I will show you every day. Never taking you for granted."

Tears pricked her eyes and she nodded. She blew out a breath and wrapped Xander in a hug. Once her tears dried, she pulled back and watched as Xander stood, offering his hand.

"We should have Liv look you over."

She nodded and took his hand, smiling when he pulled her close.

"Please, don't ever leave me again. If I'm being dense or a dumbass, just punch me in the face. Trust me, it would be less painful."

Her cheeks heated with embarrassment and she nodded. "I promise. I won't ever leave you."

Chapter Nine

Xander

Xander opened the door and groaned aloud when several voices drifted up to them.

Over the years since Liv had gotten her own lab, Kai and Ghost had added medical equipment and a triage section, so she could fix any odd injuries from an assignment. Liv had also self-trained, reading as many medical journals and any information she could find and even studied with a doctor to obtain emergency medical experience, detailed anatomy lessons, and tips that she couldn't glean from a book. It was enough knowledge that she could perform surgeries with skill.

She had said that the more she understood human anatomy and their blood on a cellular level, then she could solve the differences between humans and immortals, and yet, the answers still eluded her.

Xander turned to Frost and watched as she smiled back at him.

She had grown close to the others over the past few weeks, especially when he'd been researching code from breaking into computer systems. He loved how they welcomed her as though she'd always been a part of them.

She led the way downstairs, and he could tell when she had been spotted because Jade squealed a second before Frost was enveloped in a tight hug. Frost chuckled and hugged her back.

Jade ushered Frost to the exam table and easily lifted her up on it, treating her as if she were the most delicate being. Xander moved when Frost had, and stood by the table and reached for her hand.

Liv, impatient to know more, pushed everyone out of the way and came to stand in front of the two nervous parents.

"May I?"

When Frost nodded, Liv uncovered her stomach and there was a collective gasp from around the room. His gaze was on his mate's swollen belly.

How had I missed this?

Several emotions ran through him, but nothing as prominent as how proud he was of his mate. He leaned down to kiss her, needing the connection.

"Are you happy?"

"More than I've ever been in my life. I'm so glad I finally found you," he admitted.

The next few minutes were a whirlwind. Liv drew her blood and set Frost up to perform an ultrasound.

The room grew silent as Liv adjusted the picture of the baby on the monitor. They all stared as the barely developed feet and hands of the baby came into focus. Xander felt his heart beat hard in his chest at the sight and pressed a kiss to Frost's forehead, keeping his eyes on the image the entire time.

Although they could hear the faint sound with their enhanced hearing, Liv turned on the sound and their baby's heartbeat echoed throughout the lab as everyone gathered around the monitor. None of the immortals had ever believed that a baby was possible. Hell, Xander hadn't even thought about protection whenever they made love, but he would forever feel a flare of happiness knowing that he'd been a part of bringing this little being into this world.

After checking and double-checking, Liv glanced up and met Frost's gaze. "You're about eight weeks along."

"When will he be due?"

Liv patted her hand and Frost melted against him, relaxing at the vampire's reassurance.

"It's only a guess. But since you were already a half-shifter, your pregnancy schedule will be similar to a snow leopard's gestation cycle, so your little boy will be born in three and a half months."

Xander's eyes widened and he turned to look at Frost. Most parents had much more time to prepare for a baby, but that didn't bother him. He knew Frost would make a great mom and he would try to be a great dad, but he was curious about something else.

"We're having a boy?"

"I don't know for sure. But I have a sense that our baby is a boy, yes."

He couldn't keep the goofy smile off his face. Until Frost gasped and turned to Liv, gripping the vampire's forearms and pulling her closer.

"What does this accelerated growth mean for him?"

Liv smiled in reassurance. "He will be perfectly fine. I estimate that he'll be similar to Reaper and Xander. Bitten before they had become adults and they developed normally until they became of age. For some reason, when the shifter becomes an adult, the stasis takes over and they don't age beyond that moment. He will grow up like any other baby and will be as immortal as the rest of them, but his full stasis won't kick in until he's of age."

They both relaxed at the news.

Xander wasn't the first to sense the sun starting to rise, but he knew that the vampires would need to retire soon. He wanted to take Frost home and download all the books on pregnancy he could find, even though their little man wasn't going to arrive on a human timeline. He still needed any information he could get.

"Are you showing any other physical symptoms linked to pregnancy?" Liv asked.

What symptoms?

I had to pee, a lot, for the past two nights. Didn't you notice that I got out of bed every two hours?

Yeah, but you always came back. Until tonight, but I didn't think much about it.

Frost laughed, her nose wrinkled at him. He found it endearing.

"What symptoms?"

"Sore breasts?"

Frost shook her head.

"Fatigue?"

"Nothing serious."

"Morning sickness?"

Frost flinched but shook her head.

"Heightened sense of smell?"

"Don't think so. But I'm new to this shifter thing."

"Cramps that spread out from your stomach?"

"Nope."

"Strange dreams?"

"Nah."

"Spotting?"

"No."

Frost glanced at him and he turned his full attention to her. *I have been increasingly horny.*

And with that, he picked her up and started up the stairs.

Liv's voice carried up to them when he had her halfway up the stairs. "Where are you going?"

"We'll be back over tonight." Xander paused for a moment before a question popped into his head. "Will claiming Frost do anything to harm her or the baby?"

"No. She already transitioned."

"What about sex? Is it safe for her?"

Axel chuckled before the others joined in, but he smiled when Frost giggled against his chest.

"Yes, perfectly healthy."

"Thanks. Later."

Xander ran home faster than he ever thought possible, with Frost laughing the entire way home.

Chapter Ten

Xander

Xander unlocked the door and carried Frost through, making sure to lock the door and arm the system. He started toward the stairs and up to their bedroom. Her moan stopped him on the first step as her arousal struck him and he glanced down at her.

Her eyes flashed with desire and her hands fisted the shirt he had hastily donned when he realized that Frost wasn't asleep next to him, or anywhere in the house for that matter. He knew that her desire matched his own, and now he was free to express his feelings without his own strict restrictions.

She tilted her head toward the solid oak dining room table. "Now, Xander. I can't wait."

He nodded, shifting her to one arm so he could reach for two couch pillows, before making his way the short distance. He sucked in a harsh breath when her mouth latched onto his neck and marked his skin with teasing bites and heavy suction. Something about the action made his body heat and his cock press harder against the front panel of his jeans, the denim uncomfortable against his bare skin. When he reached the table, making sure that he didn't trip over his own feet from the overwhelming sensations rippling through his body at her touch, he laid the pillows on the table. He lowered Frost down until both her head and her hips were cushioned against the softness.

But it seemed gentle wasn't what his mate was after.

Frost reached for him at the same time she wrapped her legs around his waist, pulling him closer. "If you don't rip off my clothes and slide your cock deep inside me in the next thirty seconds, I will fuck you on the kitchen floor."

Xander, sensing that her need had flared during the short distance they'd traveled, did exactly as she asked. It took only a few seconds after she growled for him to make quick work of her clothes. He rubbed his thumb over her clit before moving it lower, finding her wet heat coating his digit. Unable to stay away from her heat, he sank his thumb inside her and growled when she clenched against his flesh. When he removed his slick thumb, he sucked her sweetness off before his hands opened on her hips and pulled her closer. He lined his cock up with her entrance and pressed deep inside, savoring the entire experience, until he was fully seated inside her. His chest heaved with deep breaths and he closed his eyes for a moment, loving that his mate could bring him to the brink with little else than a demand.

He started to thrust at a pace that had her growl at him in frustration, but she felt so good clenched around his cock, preventing him from moving more than several inches at a time.

Frost clawed at his back and drove her hips up to meet his, riding his cock, until she pinned him with her bright blue-green gaze, and he lost all control. His next thrust rattled the table underneath them as the low, nearly obscene moan escaped from her lips. The sound encouraged him to drive harder into her tight, hot pussy and he reached for the edge of the table, giving him enough leverage to hit the exact spot she needed.

He was taken by surprise when her first orgasm struck. She clenched down on his cock so hard that he had to close his eyes and concentrated on his breathing to prevent his impending orgasm from overwhelming him. The mewls and curses that escaped her throat had him clutching the table harder, listening to the creak of the wood under his hands.

The slight pinch from her nails digging into his back sent pleasure straight to his cock and he jumped inside her, drawing another moan from deep in her throat. When she relaxed and slumped back on the table, he shifted his hips back and groaned as she moved her hands to clutch his forearms, pressing her hips up to meet every one of his thrusts. She released the sexiest fucking sound he'd ever heard and he wanted to draw that sound from her for the rest of their existence.

"More, Xander. Fuck me."

He still held back, gentling his thrusts as he resumed. He noticed that her entire body was shaking, and he didn't want to do anything that would hurt her.

"Harder. Take me hard."

Xander trusted Frost to tell him if he was too rough and he didn't have enough strength to hold back any longer. With his next thrust, he held her hips steady and drove into her until he felt completely absorbed by her. He loved that she clawed his skin and screamed his name as he continued his relentless pounding. He lost himself in the sensations that only his mate, the woman he truly loved, drew from him.

Not relenting, his hips drove forward until she threw her head back and screamed his name. Her second orgasm ripped through her body. Unable to hold off any longer, he closed his eyes and savored the pulsing of his cock deep inside her; he let go and followed her into blissful oblivion.

It took him several minutes to come back to reality and the first thing he spotted was her exposed neck. Her muscles had gone limp and he smiled as he watched her chest heave up and down with deep breaths. He was still burrowed deep inside her, so when he leaned forward and took a long lick where her neck curved near the collarbone, she moaned and clamped down on his still hard cock.

His teeth elongated without a thought, and he bit down, expelling his venom deep in her system. The act drew another long moan from her throat as she clutched him closer. When he felt his venom slow, he readied himself to extract his teeth and lick the wound closed, but Frost tensed and he felt her orgasm wash over his cock as she released for the third time.

Moaning, he removed his teeth slowly and licked the wound closed, before he gathered her into his arms. "Are you okay, sweetheart?"

"I'm perfect." Her words were slurred with sleep and she burrowed her face closer to his neck.

"I should have done it sooner. I will never take you for granted again."

Frost's energy completely waned and she needed sleep. He remembered the conversation about the last few nights and he vowed to take care of her. He carried her upstairs to their room, pulled back the covers, and laid her gently on the bed. He made his way to the bathroom and, after soaking a washcloth in warm water, brought it back to the bedroom. His blood surged as he roamed over her flushed skin and the smile that tilted up her mouth. He moved the cloth over her with gentle care, before he tossed it through to the open bathroom door and lay down next to her. She cuddled against his side, her head on his chest, as he wrapped her close.

"Next time, you can claim me."

He ran his fingers over the healed puncture marks that would slowly start to darken over the coming days. But they would always remain. He smiled when she shivered at his touch.

"I would love to." Her mouth moved on his skin.

"Have you thought about a name for our son?" The surge of happiness that thrummed through his body at the thought of his mate carrying his son wouldn't dampen any time soon. Frost was everything he would ever want, and now, his son as well.

"Nothing comes to mind."

"I've always been partial to the name Silas. What do you think?"

Frost gasped and with Xander's hand on her belly, he could feel when the baby moved inside her. But what he hadn't been expecting was the wave of happiness that struck him a moment later. Frost laughed as Xander looked at her with awe, and they stroked her belly together.

"Well, Silas loves it. Maybe now he'll let me sleep and leave my bladder alone," she joked.

Another wave of feeling washed over them. This time it was contentment along with the happiness. Before long, Xander could hear Frost's deep breathing. And he could've sworn that he fell asleep with a smile on his face as sleep claimed him several minutes later.

<u>Chapter Eleven</u>

Frost

Hunter and Gunnar sat cross-legged on the floor next to Frost, who leaned back against the couch. She snuggled between Xander's thighs as he sat on the couch, a computer on his lap and his fingers flying over the keyboard. Gunnar and Hunter were talking to Silas. She smiled as her and Xander's son got to know each of the assassins in his own way. She had now seen a side of these intense men that she never thought possible.

Although they had been there during the ultrasound, each of the men had continued to call Silas a miracle and acted in awe by the fact that she was pregnant. And she understood. Even immortals couldn't impregnate a human, because as Liv explained it, it was biologically impossible. They still didn't understand how she had fallen pregnant, but Liv, armed with the explanation about her skin glowing and shifter mixes being extremely rare, believed that they were somehow able to pause Xander's stasis long enough for her to conceive. Frankly, all the science made her head hurt, but she enjoyed each moment of carrying Xander's baby.

Over the past three weeks, Silas had grown at a healthy rate as her belly expanded, until Liv told her she was a little shy of eighteen weeks pregnant, in human terms. During the time she and Xander spent alone with Silas, they tried to establish communication with him through a mind link, but so far, Silas had remained silent. They only cared that he was growing and healthy, which Liv assured Frost of whenever the latter would show up in the vampire's lab with a concerned look on her face. Between her still frequent trips to the restroom, falling asleep wherever she sat and whatever time she wanted, and the baby bump she carried, there were no other symptoms that she and Xander had both read about.

The assassins had sensed Silas the moment Frost had come to Liv for answers, and each of them spent time with Silas in their own way. Xander read it was important for Silas to know the voices of those he would be close to in order to form a bond. After he explained that to the group, they immediately cornered Frost and started talking to Silas, with no hesitation. So every day, after Xander made her a large breakfast, her first of several meals for the day, they wandered over to Kai and Liv's to spend time with their family.

Silas had also become stronger as he grew, throwing out waves of emotions, his way of communicating without talking. The assassins would know how Silas reacted to a story by the emotions they would feel from him. But the best reaction Silas had was whenever Xander was near. Silas would sense him and practically tap dance in her belly until Xander pressed his hands to her skin, and then he would calm and send out radiating waves of happiness. And each night since they learned of Silas, Xander would sleep wrapped around her, his hands settled on her stomach, allowing both Silas and herself to sleep through the night.

"Do you think you'll look like your mommy? Dark hair and blue-green eyes? Or your daddy, with white hair and blue eyes?" Gunnar asked.

They had been curious as to what combination of features Silas would have. Silas thought it was funny because he didn't know what he looked like, much less an image of Frost and Xander, and sent out waves of confusion, but he felt included and that made him happy. And that, in turn, made Xander and her happy.

As Frost went to rub her tummy, a loud voice in her head stopped her movements and she felt Xander's hand squeeze her shoulder in reaction.

Daddy!

There was a rush of movement throughout the house as the immortals flooded the living room, all looking at her. That was when she realized that Silas had mind linked with everyone, at the same time, not just her and Xander, which was a feat by itself.

Frost laughed as she ran comforting circles around her belly. "Of course you would say Daddy first."

Daddy!

Xander moved the laptop aside and leaned down. He ran his

hand underneath her shirt and touched her skin. "I'm here, little man."

Silas giggled at that, but soon settled inside her, comforted by the fact that Xander was still close. Gunnar and Hunter continued talking as if they hadn't been interrupted by a baby in the womb speaking to the lot of them without any hesitation. Frost laughed and shook her head. She loved her life.

The front door opened and Jade walked in carrying a large box. "Did I just hear Silas?"

Frost nodded and chuckled at her shocked face. Jade dropped the box onto the coffee table and kneeled in front of her. "Hi Silas, it's your Aunt Jade and she missed you."

Silas sent out a wave of affection for Jade.

Frost patted her on the cheek. "You're going to be such a great aunt."

At that time, Kai came from the kitchen with Liv, and he handed Frost a sandwich she had forgotten about asking for. She was certain she had mumbled it under her breath, but of course, Kai heard it.

"Thank you, Kai."

When she lifted the slice of bread covered in mayonnaise and mustard, she couldn't help the smile that bloomed on her face or that her stomach rumbled loudly for everyone to hear. The sandwich was just as she asked for. Thinly sliced turkey topped with an inch of peanut butter—chunky, of course—and a generous sprinkling of red chile sauce. And on the side, a bowl of pickle spears dunked in cottage cheese.

"No problem. What's in the box?" Kai circled it, automatically suspicious.

Frost shrugged, not really caring one way or the other, and dug into her sandwich. She knew that she was making obscene sounds while eating, but she couldn't help it—she was hungry all the time and the food tasted so good. Silas hummed as she ate, and within minutes, she had demolished the sandwich and her sides, while everyone looked at her as though she were an alien who had sprouted wings. She captured Seth's hand after he set down a large glass of milk in front of her and squeezed as her way of thanking him. Xander chuckled at the reaction from the others each time she ate, but she laid her head back against his stomach as the food coma set in, too satisfied to care.

"Although it looks and smells disgusting, I can't taste a trace of it when I kiss her."

The front door opened again and Axel walked in, buck naked, and shut the door behind him casually. He walked toward the one unoccupied chair and went to sit down, but Kai snarled at him, a vicious sound that, if it were directed at her, she would pee herself. Frost, who sat closest to the stash of clothing, opened the top lid of the ottoman and grabbed out a pair of sweats. She threw them to Ax, who donned them and then sat down with a defiant smile aimed toward Kai.

Ghost, Reaper, Ara, and Aubrey all came in. They said their hellos to Silas, and her baby greeted each of them by saying hi to them through their mind link. It was hilarious as they froze, all staring at her belly with wide, disbelieving eyes.

"Who brought the box?" Liv arrived silently from her lab and darted to Kai's side.

"It was on the doorstep addressed to Frost, so I brought it in when I arrived," Jade said.

She had gone to the kitchen and grabbed the leftover pasta that Frost had wanted for an after-meal snack. Although the shifters had a large appetite, it was nothing compared to Frost at that moment. She eyed Jade and the pasta when Jade sat next to her, but when she let a growl slip through her lips, Jade scooted a couple of feet away and dug in.

Distracting herself from the food she missed out on, she struggled to stand until Xander lifted her up, and she waddled over to see what was in the box. Silas had settled down from all the excitement and conversation, and as she approached the box, she felt some trepidation. No one truly knew she was here, or knew that she had found a mate in Xander. She had ordered a crib and wondered whether they had misread the address or whether she had been the one to make the mistake. But she grew nervous when she glanced around and couldn't find a shipping label on the box, just a card taped haphazardly to the side.

Ripping the card off, she opened the envelope. As she dug it out, her eyes spotted the signature. Anzû. So he knew that Xander would figure out the links between the mercenaries and his company, Nightfall. She dropped the card onto the floor and stepped back quickly from the box.

Instantly alert, the other's in the room closed in on the box as Frost moved away. Silas picked up on her distress and with the sensations tingling through her, she could feel that he put an invisible barricade around the box.

"Huh. Well, Silas put a barrier around the box and he won't let anyone near it."

Ara stepped forward and placed her hand on Frost's stomach. "Silas, I can open the box in your protective bubble if you let me in."

Okay.

Ara's eyes widened as she was able to open the box with the barrier still in place, and Frost blew out a relieved breath. But confusion and fear swamped her as Ara lifted a bouncer with a colorful pinwheel suspended above it.

"Destroy it." Frost's voice dropped to a deadly whisper.

Ara immediately crushed it and then managed to pulverize it until there was nothing but dust left, which she put back in the box and closed it.

"Silas, can you remove your barrier so I can take the box outside?" Kai reached for it slowly and when he gripped the side, he walked the box out the front door, taking it somewhere out of sight, before coming back in. He shut and locked the door.

From the corner of her eye, she spotted Xander pick up the note from the floor. "He must've had us surveilled from a distance, enough to know that Frost is pregnant by sight alone."

"What does the note say?" Her curiosity got the better of her.

"I'll see you soon. P.S. Tell Ghost I said hi."

<u>Chapter Twelve</u>

Xander

There had been no further activity from Anzû or any of his shifters since they'd received the note the month before. It had been decided that the assassins, much like when they were protecting Ara, would stick close to Xander's house, a sort of protection detail. They were in close quarters until they found out what Anzû truly wanted and stopped him or destroyed him once and for all.

Xander had found that he couldn't be apart from Frost for very long. One, because he didn't want to, but when he did, Silas would send out a wave of unhappiness until Xander came close. It would upset Frost, and he hated to see Frost upset.

Xander had been working overtime trying to find a connection between anyone in the government, to see whether they had an off-books connection with Nightfall. Although the company was relatively new, Xander had found some redacted material about an old, defunct company that Anzû had been connected to, albeit loosely. The company had been fired while under contract with the government, but there was no information on who owned them or the name of the employees under them. Apparently whatever they had done had Anzû and the company banned from ever being contracted by the government again. The information had been deleted or someone just as talented as Xander had moved it to a private server so no one could ever find it.

Ghost's contact was told that as long as Dark Company existed, they wouldn't have a need for another immortal assassin group. But if Anzû knew that he was banned, he might believe the only way to get a government contract was to kill the assassins and take over, hopefully without much scrutiny. The one thing that made no sense was his fascination with Frost. Anzû knew that Frost wasn't his mate; it would be obvious to any self-respecting immortal to understand and leave another's mate alone. But he persisted with little thought for failure. Which, if he continued, would happen, because Xander would kill him if the fucker came close to Frost.

Xander knew that she was powerful, transitioning without the effect of his venom and she could speak through their mind link quicker than any other of the other immortal mates had, without even knowing it was possible. And now Silas, in the womb, could mind link with any immortal he wanted to, on top of being able to put an effective barrier around any person or thing he wanted. They had gone so far as to test the strength of his established barrier; and not one of the immortals could make a dent, much less was able to break it. Silas had told them that he didn't have to think about it. If he wanted it, it appeared.

And that was another thing that awed them. Silas could effectively communicate with complete sentences. Among his other talents, he had emotional ones as well. He could sense auras and send out emotions to reassure or strengthen someone's existing feelings. Both his son and his mate were brilliant.

Xander had spent another night working all the way until morning after getting a lead on Anzû, and happened to stumble upon a photo of him. He had showed the picture to those who had gathered around their house, but no one recognized the shifter.

Daddy?

Xander rushed up the stairs toward Frost and carried her the rest of the way down the stairs and onto the couch. He kissed her before he kneeled, slipped his hand underneath Frost's shirt, and rubbed her stomach.

"How are you, little man?"

Frost's stomach protruded even more. He remembered that Liv mentioned the day before that Frost looked eight months pregnant and Silas's growth was perfect.

You've been gone too long. Mommy couldn't sleep.

"I'm done now. We'll take a nap later together, how does that sound?"

Silas sent out a wave of happiness that made both him and Frost smile. Thomas gave back the picture that Xander had passed around and Xander handed it to Frost. "Do you recognize him?"

"Yes." Her words were rushed and before their next breath, Silas had put up a barrier around the three of them. "It's okay, baby. It's okay. We're okay."

Her words relaxed Silas and he dropped the barriers.

"He was at the diner the morning we set off and then we ran into him on the second day, but he never spoke to us or seemed to know any of the mercenaries who were with me. He walked away soon after I spotted him."

Ghost walked in and made a beeline for him, and glanced down at the photo. "I remember him. He's a bear shifter who came to me for a job about a half century ago. He had just transitioned and believed that all we did was kill people for fun and he wanted to be a part of it. I told him that I didn't have a spot for him and he became so volatile that he trashed my office. I haven't seen him since."

"It still doesn't explain what he wants with Frost and he knows that we, as a group, are too powerful to win an all-out battle, no matter how many he's recruited. We should assume the worst and keep our eyes open."

Silas, barrier please.

Yes, Mommy.

They had taught Silas to put a barrier around himself, blocking both sounds and thoughts, until Frost hummed a certain note that vibrated against the barrier, letting Silas know it was safe to listen again.

"I don't care what the fuck he wants. If he goes anywhere near Silas, I will rip his fucking throat out." With that, she waddled toward the kitchen. *Xander.*

When he arrived in the kitchen, she had removed the lasagna from the fridge, leftovers from the dinner the night before, and he took the pan and cut her a large piece. He went to the fridge to see what they had, because she wouldn't eat the pasta alone. "Do you want whipped cream, marshmallow fluff, pickles, cream cheese, or mustard?"

"Yes."

He turned to her and raised his eyebrow, but Frost pierced him with a glare that had him shivering. He topped her lasagna and put everything away when she was happy with her breakfast. But halfway through her meal, she paused with her fork near her mouth, before she set it back down on her plate. He wondered, for a split second, whether she had gone into labor, but then her arousal reached his senses. Although they'd had sporadic moments alone, they had spent every night together, well, except for the night before. With those crowding in the house and him busy working finding any leads he could, it didn't leave them much time for sex.

Frost reached for him and pulled him down in a heated kiss and he swallowed her loud moan. He wrapped his arms around her and lost himself to the sensations of his mate and her talented mouth.

"Please make love to me." It was a demand and a request.

Her body vibrated with a need that matched his own. Xander lifted her in his arms, loving the weight of his mate and their son, and walked toward the living room.

"Everyone out. We'll be fine on our own for the day. You can come back tonight."

Xander ushered everyone toward the door, waiting for Ax to make a smart-ass remark, and smiled when, as he opened his mouth, Xander slammed the door in his face and locked it. He armed the system and ran upstairs, all of this with Frost pressed close to his chest. He gently lowered her onto the bed and with deft movements, ripped her clothing off her. He stood, amazed at her round belly and the fact that this woman, his mate, loved him.

"Please."

He quickly discarded his clothing. He laid down on the bed next to her and turned her onto her side. When she was comfortable, he lay behind her, pressing his chest to her back, and wrapped his arms around her. His mouth found the sensitive part of her neck, just below her ear, and started nipping at it. He shivered as she moaned at the sensations.

His hands weren't idle. He ran his fingers along her throat before he caressed lower, drawing sexy moans from her wherever he touched her. She gasped as he tweaked her nipple, holding it between his thumb and forefinger and squeezed, adding only a little pressure.

"Fuck, Xander. More."

"I love how you experience pleasure. And the words that come from your mouth drive me crazy."

Another rush of scent washed over him and unable to stay away, he ran his hands down until his fingers rested on her clit. He flicked the sensitized nub until she cried out with her first orgasm. He coated his fingers with her release and brought his hand to his mouth, sucking her sweet taste off his fingers.

"I need your cock. Now."

"Oh, God, sweetheart. I'm going to fuck you until you come all over my hard, pounding cock."

The moan that escaped her throat had him harden further, if that were even possible. With quick movements, he lifted her leg and draped it over his hip, exposing her and allowing him to press forward with ease. Moving his fingers back to her clit, he waited until she cried out from the ongoing sensations from her over-sensitized nub before he slid deep inside her with one thrust. His other arm slipped underneath her and held her tight to his body as he started to move. The vibrations of her first orgasm still coursed through her and with every thrust, she panted his name and begged for more.

"It's been too long."

"Sweetheart...I took you yesterday in the shower...and then again in my office." He panted as the pleasure started to overwhelm him.

"I know, but that was yesterday. I need you."

"You have me, sweetheart. You always will."

She rocked back against him as he drove his hips forward, finding a rhythm that had both of them keening as her orgasm approached. With one hand pinching her nipples and the other rubbing circles against her clit, she pressed back against him and cried out. Her muscles clamped down on his cock as her come washed over him.

The sudden pressure and her wetness had him shouting her name as he buried himself deep inside and let go.

The pulse of his cock had her shivering against him, and another wave of pleasure washed over her. For the next few seconds, she squeezed every ounce of come from him.

This time, it took him a few minutes to catch his breath. He could feel her shaking from the intensity of their lovemaking, and he held her tightly, kissing her neck until her shivers subsided and she fell limp against him.

"I love you, Xander."

"I love you, too, sweetheart."

Surprise shook him when she wiggled out of his grasp, but when she pushed him onto his back and crawled on his lap, he opened his mouth to protest. That protest died when she sank down on his still hard cock, drawing a groan from both of them. He had closed his eyes, but they flew open when Frost licked a swath near his collarbone. He sucked in a breath when he watched as her teeth elongated for the first time since she'd transitioned. She leaned forward, and without hesitation, pierced his skin with her teeth and released her venom into his bloodstream. The pleasure from her bite was so great, he gripped Frost's hips and kept her hips flush with his as he released for a second time deep inside her.

When she pulled back and sealed his punctures with a lick, she rocked her hips against his and he reached for her clit again. With all the sensations swirling around him, Frost's release rocked him to his core. She dropped down onto his chest, and he held her for the longest time. He savored this quiet moment with her, until her body sagged with exhaustion. He laid her down and propped her belly with a body pillow to relieve some of the pressure on her back, and turned to face her.

They were quiet for a long while, thinking about everything and nothing as they savored this time together.

"You know when they find out about Silas, Anzû and his goons will target him."

"Why do you think that?" Xander felt fear chill him to the bone.

"Because he's unique, and people who crave power collect what's unique. Their dedication to power gives them an advantage."

Xander shook his head. "I won't allow that to happen. Our family won't allow that to happen."

Frost sensed his panic, because she smiled and ran her hands over her stomach. "I'm going to miss being this close to him." She hummed and they both felt his barrier fall. Silas sensed their tension and sent out waves of contentment and happiness. Frost laughed and rubbed her belly.

"We love you, too, baby."

As they relaxed into sleep, Xander made a promise to himself that he would protect them, no matter how far he had to go to do it.

<u>Chapter Thirteen</u>

Frost

Frost waddled from the kitchen after having demolished a sandwich, an entire pie topped with hot sauce, and a vanilla milkshake. During her pregnancy, chocolate made her sick to her stomach, much to her disappointment. She walked through the doorway and turned slightly so that her bump wouldn't hit and groaned when she heard the others in the living room as they chuckled at her predicament. She casually flipped them off, which only made them laugh harder, as she finally made it through.

The past month had been quiet, no word from Anzû or anyone else. The assassins quietly left for jobs that popped up here and there, but for the most part, they stuck close, waiting for the moment Silas would be introduced to the world. It had been relaxing, except for the fact that she ate everything in sight mixed with condiments she didn't even know existed until Xander had gone to the store and bought one of everything he found. She and Silas slept quite a bit, on the couch or an armchair if she couldn't be bothered to head upstairs to bed. Although she had read about the symptoms of pregnancy and Liv had asked her, almost weekly, about everything from tender breasts to morning sickness, the cravings and sleep were all that were different now. But she could understand her cravings. Her shifter mix genes, along with feeding Silas, who grew so quickly, made her hungry at almost hour intervals.

She snarled at the group as she walked closer, but paused when she felt a warm gush between her legs. Only a second later, she doubled over as her first contraction struck.

"Liv?" She choked.

Xander came from somewhere in the house and wrapped a comforting arm around her, taking her weight easily, while he rubbed circles on her back with his other hand.

"Is it time?" Liv sounded calm until she glanced down and spotted what had alarmed Frost in the first place. Then she sprang into action. "Seth, fill the tub and get the medical supplies."

The contraction passed and she was able to stand with Xander's help. When she glanced up, she couldn't help the bark of laughter that erupted from her throat. Around her, the most capable and deadly assassins in the world sat frozen as they stared at her.

"Baby, you'll be here soon, but I think we broke your aunts and uncles."

"Are you in pain, sweetheart?"

She shook her head. "Not now that the contraction has passed.

It's been thirty seconds. Could you count until the next one?"

"No pain then?"

"Just pressure." She groaned. "Well, it's a heavy pressure and a little pain."

Seth appeared at the top of the stairs. "Everything's ready."

She took a step, but blew out a relieved breath when Xander picked her up and carried her toward the stairs. Before he was halfway across the living room, the assassins snapped out of their stupor and made to follow them, but stopped in their tracks when Xander growled a warning.

"Not a fucking chance, especially Ax. Not one of you will see Frost naked, even while giving birth. Sit back down."

Ax looked a little put out, but when she moaned as the next contraction took hold, he immediately took his seat on the couch. Jade walked toward them and gave her a kiss on the cheek.

"You'll do great, girlfriend." Jade rubbed Frost's stomach, and the pain eased a little with her touch. "You too, little man."

Losing patience, Xander turned and rushed upstairs, taking care not to jar her. Which, at that point, didn't matter anyway because the contractions hurt like a son of a bitch. Not that she would admit that out loud and freak Xander out. When they reached the master bathroom, Liv and Seth stood by the side of the tub as Xander lowered her in. He waited until she leaned back against some bath pillows he bought for the occasion, before stripping off her pants and underwear, leaving her naked from the waist down.

As the feeling of the warm water surrounded her and Silas, she took a deep breath as the buoyancy of the water relieved some of the pressure. But another contraction hit just as she tried to relax in the tub. She ignored it when Liv clambered over the tub and sank down on her knees in front of Frost, examining her. Frost's breath rushed out when a particularly strong compression had her biting her lip, preventing the curse from slipping out.

"Okay sweetie, this is going to be quick. Silas is ready." Liv tried to sound encouraging.

Frost was swamped with anxiety as Silas heard and understood his Aunt Liv's words. She rubbed her hands over her belly and relaxed back, but the tub and the pillows weren't cutting it. Xander sensed this and crawled into the tub, placing himself between Frost and the hard surface, and immediately Silas sent relieved waves of happiness throughout the room.

"Thank…you."

"I would do anything for you. This is nothing, sweetheart. I'm sorry I can't take the pain from you."

Leaning against his shoulder, she tilted her head to the side so she could look at Xander. "You gave us a son, and I'm willing to endure anything for him. Are you ready?"

Xander's searing kiss was enough of an answer that when the kiss ended, she turned back to Liv, determined. On the next contraction, which was now timed at exactly three minutes apart, she nodded at Liv, ready for instructions. Her eyes darted up and watched Seth prepare the tray in case of a C-section, but she purposely ignored it when another wave of pain struck.

Time stopped having meaning and the moments became blurred as the throbbing pain pulled her out of her own consciousness. She managed to reassure Silas that she wasn't in pain, encouraging Xander to speak to him, because he always calmed when his daddy talked to him. She also managed to bite back most of the curses that wanted to slip through her clenched teeth, but a few slipped through when she had been too far gone to care.

When Liv finally asked her to push, it had been a relief. She was an immortal, but giving birth was painful at the best of times. Other times, she felt as though she was being split in half and didn't know how she would survive. But after being asked several times to push, the pain in her body lessened and she concentrated on Liv as she asked her to bear down once more.

There was a flurry of activity, but her eyes had closed when Liv had told her that she did so well. She leaned back and savored being wrapped in Xander's arms. As she relaxed back, her muddled brain cleared slightly and she realized that she hadn't heard Silas cry.

"Xander?"

He gave her a look that she couldn't identify. "You were amazing, sweetheart. We have a son."

Mommy?

A relieved breath escaped her sore throat.

Liv appeared in front of her with her son. She reached for Silas, grateful that Xander supported her arms with his. "He's beautiful. The most beautiful baby ever." Liv's voice choked with emotion and Frost noticed tears in her eyes.

Frost glanced down at her son in her arms and fell completely and utterly in love with her little man in that moment. He had a shock of white hair that matched Xander's perfectly. He had the same olive skin, not the pale complexion that she had. His lips were full, like hers, but his nose belonged to Xander. He was perfect in every way.

"You look exactly like Daddy."

Xander reached out and traced a finger down his hair and onto his cheek, and Silas leaned into his touch and sighed. "Hey, little man. I'm so happy you're here."

Daddy!

Silas blinked open his eyes and they both gasped at their first glimpse at the color of his eyes. They were ice-blue, but green flecks were sprinkled throughout. They reminded her of an exploded star, both beautiful and dangerous. "He's perfect."

Liv and Seth walked over to look at their son, who smiled up at them, and they were just as taken aback as she was when they spotted his unique eyes. They all stared at Silas as he stared back at them, fascinated.

"That's your Aunt Liv and Uncle Seth." Again, a smile brightened his face.

"How are you doing, Frost?"

"I'm good. Tired and a little sore, but I feel that my body is already healing." She put one hand on her now empty belly and felt tears prick her eyes.

"He's right here, sweetheart. Silas will always be a part of you."

Xander kissed her softly before wiping away the tears that fell at his words.

She squeezed Silas closer. He let out a contented sound and blinked up at them, his eyes refusing to look away from his parents. Xander's arms came around them both.

As she watched, her little man grew more and more tired.

"I promise to do everything in my power to protect my two men who I love most in this world."

After she finished the last word, the three of them glowed bright before the light faded away from their skin. Their bond had been recognized and in her mind, was completely binding, forever.

Chapter Fourteen

Xander

Frost had fallen asleep as soon as he tucked her in bed. He had kissed her forehead, loving the smile that touched her lips, and listened for a long while as her breathing became deep and even. While she slept, Xander couldn't tear his eyes away from his son who slept in his crib about a foot from the bed. His son's hair was whiter than his own and so soft to the touch. Xander could see his eyes dart back and forth behind his thin eyelids and every so often, he would clench his little hands into a fist and scrunch his face as though he were about to cry, but then settled back into sleep.

Silas was perfect in every way, and yet Xander felt that this tiny being he and Frost were responsible for, who they loved more than life itself, was so small and fragile. So while Frost got much needed sleep, Xander's emotions had swung between fear and awe as he stared at his sleeping son.

Being an immortal for as long as he had, Xander had forgotten the impressive talents and qualities that each immortal brought to the forefront when they transitioned. He should've thought about it when Silas had spoken to everyone through his mind link, and it should have surprised him, but he thought it was a normal part of everyday life. But as he looked at Silas, he realized that he was special. He was more powerful than they could understand, but Xander wanted him to have as normal a life as he possibly could. With family surrounding him and knowing that he was loved.

Being a parent hadn't terrified him until he spotted Silas for the first time, but he knew he wouldn't fail with Frost by his side. He loved his family and protectiveness surged through him. He would do everything in his power to protect them.

Sometime during the night, he had fallen asleep and cradled Frost to his chest. In the early morning hours, he had sensed more than he heard her breathing change, and he squeezed her closer.

"This is probably a dumb question, but how are you feeling?"

Frost smiled and kissed him. Xander savored the kiss and her taste. She moved onto her back and stretched her arms and legs before she sat up. "Good. There's no pain or tenderness anymore. I think I'm well on my way to being completely healed. How's Silas?"

"He's good. He settled down to sleep rather quickly. I hear him stirring now."

With one last kiss, Xander scrambled out of bed and helped Frost up before they glanced down at their son in his crib. Silas was on his back, staring up at the mobile above his bed with a mix of curiosity and confusion. As they moved closer, Silas turned his concentration on both of them.

Mommy! Daddy!

Frost scooped him up and cuddled him close, before placing him down on the changing table. The next few minutes had them learning how to change a diaper and struggling to put him in a onesie that would keep him warm. Xander, only admitting it to himself, thought the outfit looked cute on his son. Silas didn't seem too affected by any of the changes he had been introduced to.

"You okay, little man?"

I'm fine, Daddy.

He couldn't help but smile at how mature his newborn son sounded. Xander had him in his arms after they changed him and he glanced at Frost, who beamed at the both of them.

"Ready to head downstairs?"

"Yeah. Let's go before they combust with excitement to meet our little man." Frost shook her head at the energy she could feel, even all the way upstairs.

Silas tried to look everywhere, all at once, as they headed down the stairs. Soon, he started fussing and Xander glanced down to see Jade waiting anxiously at the bottom step. Silas could sense her. Or maybe they were already talking to each other.

Xander carefully maneuvered the stairs and when he reached the living room, Jade already moved to sit on the couch, waiting to hold Silas. Xander carefully lowered Silas on to her lap. His head was cradled on her closed knees and she stared at Silas with a look of awe on her face. He knew the feeling. Of course, they had started talking with no one else clued into their conversation.

Frost was pulled into hugs, first by Kai and then the others, all congratulating them on the son each of them had become enamored with as soon as they laid eyes on him.

Soon, the others became impatient, all wanting a turn holding and talking to Silas. And their son charmed the entire group, who had their turn holding him and cooing at him. Quite a sight—an entire group of assassins could become a puddle of goo when it came to his son, but Xander was in the same boat so he didn't tease them, much.

Hungry.

Both he and Frost looked at each other. They hadn't thought that far. They looked back at Silas, this time in Liv's arms, before they looked back at each other. They had no idea what to do. A typical baby would breast feed or take a bottle, but at their son's request, they were suddenly at a loss.

"Why don't you just ask Silas what he wants to eat?" Liv provided helpfully.

Frost lifted Silas in her arms and walked toward the kitchen with him close behind. "Would you like breast milk?"

Xander could have sworn that he heard "eww" coming from Silas. Frost laughed and hugged Silas close to her. Xander loved her laugh.

He opened the cabinet they had stocked with baby food and formulas, unsure of what Silas would need, but prepared in case.

Most books recommended complementing breast milk with baby food at four to six months old, but again, Silas wasn't a typical baby. He was an immortal and only he could tell them what he would like and wouldn't like.

Frost slid Silas to her hip and Xander pulled out the formula first and got another annoyed look for their efforts. He pulled out pureed carrots, peas, apples, until he reached the pears, which Silas nodded at. Xander took Silas and placed him in his high chair as Frost opened the jar and grabbed a baby spoon. She put a tiny amount at the end of the hard plastic spoon and held it close to Silas's mouth. Without hesitation, their son opened and took the bite, humming at the taste. Frost kept feeding him little bites until the jar was empty and Silas's eyes drooped.

"Is this normal?" Xander had known Liv hovered close.

Liv shrugged. "What's normal for an immortal? This is just as much new territory for him as it was for you when you transitioned. He's the first baby born to immortal parents and because of this, you two are going to have to learn as you go. But we, all of us, are here to help."

Liv bent down and kissed Silas on the forehead and they all watched as a smile formed on his face.

"He can communicate with us, and that's more than most parents could hope for. The rest, we'll figure out, I promise."

Frost kissed Xander, smoothing away the creases that appeared on his forehead whenever he was concerned. She lifted Silas into her arms, his head settling comfortably against her shoulder, and he fell asleep.

"I don't think he liked the diapers. He was fine with the onesie, but I have a feeling that he'll want to potty train as soon as possible."

Xander smiled at Frost, who beamed back. He moved in for a fast, but intense kiss. When he pulled back, he slid his fingers through her hair, but before Xander could place another kiss on her lips, Ghost's phone rang. He didn't pay much attention to the call, but when Ghost threw the phone against the fireplace, he turned in surprise. Ghost never let anything get to him.

Silas, sensing his uncle's distress, put up his barrier that everyone could feel in the house as soon as it was created. But instead of protecting only those he could see in the kitchen and living room, he had conjured a barrier that covered the entire house. They could see the faint shimmer right outside the window and they all looked at Silas in awe.

"Ghost?" Kai sounded concerned.

Ghost shook his head and glanced at Frost, who held Silas in her arms. Ghost had melted, along with the rest of them, and now he placed his large hand over Silas's head, gently. "Anzû wants me to deliver Frost to him. He said, that in exchange, he would give us all we wanted to know about the immortals' origins."

Frost scoffed. "That stupid fucking idiot doesn't know when to quit. Like we couldn't figure that out for ourselves." She paused and glanced down at Silas. "Please don't repeat—well, just to be safe—any of the words that Mommy just said."

Silas giggled, the first time he'd done so, and Xander found himself smiling down at his son, despite the threat that had come through minutes before.

"You know Frost is the key to our origins, right?" Liv said.

Most of the group looked at Liv with a smile. Xander didn't. He wanted to know why she thought so and was grateful when she continued.

"I had an inkling when I spotted the distinct pattern in Frost's eyes and seeing Silas only confirmed my theory. I believe that the first immortals, vampire and shifter alike, were born, not created. And they were most likely born from half-human, half-immortal beings like Frost, those who didn't know they had shifter genes. She's an immortal, but her body isn't in the same stasis that mine is, or Ara's, Aubrey's, or Jade's."

"But aren't I in the same stasis that the women are?"

"And there's where I believe Frost is special. There's no way to test it, like I ever would, but if a half, or shifter mix as Frost likes to call herself, mated with another immortal mix, they could produce an immortal with powers, such as Silas has. That immortal would be able to turn others with a bite, injecting their venom into the system of humans, turning them immortal. Not all the time, though; most humans die with our venom in their system.

"I believe she was able to free you from your stasis, only for a short time, which is why she hasn't glowed since your first time. I believe that her body knows when a pregnancy is viable, and that's how she was able to become pregnant. And because Frost was able to conceive after her transition, I believe that if you chose to, Frost could have more children. But she could only have children with her mate. I can test Silas's blood when he's older, but his eyes, the combination of Frost's curious ones and Xander's, makes him unique."

They grew quiet as the group studied Silas, who had gone back to sleep during Liv's explanation.

"We're going to have to come up with a plan. Anzû's not going to stop until he gets what he wants, which is Frost and control of Dark Company."

So, for the next few hours, they settled in the living room, Silas sleeping in the arms of the immortal who wanted to hold him, as they bandied about a plan to lure Anzû to them, using home advantage when confronting him. Between Kai, Reaper, Ara, Jade, Hunter, Gunnar, Ghost, Ax, Kane, Thomas, Isaac, and himself, they had no idea how to do that without dangling Frost as bait, which Xander had vehemently refused.

They decided in the end that investigation and hunkering down was their best and only option. Jade and Gunnar would do recon on Anzû and identify any associate he had. The rest would add more sensors and cameras to their properties and would review footage in case they caught anyone they didn't recognize on camera. The sooner they ID'd the men associated with Anzû, the more they could learn about the enemy and use that information to destroy them.

Xander knew exactly where Frost and Silas were at every moment, so when they stood from making their plans, he found her laying on the couch, snuggling Silas on her chest, both sound asleep.

Anger rushed through his limbs and up his chest, before the feeling clogged his throat. He had no idea what would happen if Anzû captured Frost, but Xander would kill him before that happened. He was off his fucking rocker and they would find a way to destroy him.

Not one of the assassins had ever fought another immortal to the death. Most immortals wanted to be left alone, to do as they pleased, and learned not to kill humans and bring a spotlight on their existence. Some of them banded together, like Ghost's company, but more for companionship than survival. Anzû wasn't only jeopardizing his own family, but to pick on someone as strong as they were, he had to be crazy. And that would lead to him being destroyed.

Xander felt exhaustion over every inch of his body, so he bid everyone goodnight and lifted Frost in his arms. Her hold of Silas was secure, so he made his way up the stairs. When he reached the room, he laid Frost down first. He tucked Silas into his crib and scanned for anything in his crib that might pose a danger to him, before he kissed his son's head and joined Frost in bed.

"What are you worried about?" Frost's sleep-laden voice reached him as he lay down.

"I've been extremely lucky these past few months. Lucky to have found you and now we have Silas. But now this one shifter has threatened everything that matters to me. That's the only reason I'm thinking about ways to kill him, once and for all."

"But you aren't alone in the fight. Whatever force he has, I know you guys can defeat him. Ara, alone, is more destructive than any other immortal and you are effectively trained fighters, having an advantage even against immortals. Trust yourself and the others, and everything will be fine."

He pulled her close and kissed her. "How do you feel?"

"Every time I look at Silas, I feel a wonder that I've never experienced before. Physically, I've healed completely, but I'm still a little tired and feel like I could sleep for a week."

"I'll take care of everything until you feel better. I've never loved anyone more than I love both you and Silas. Thank you for being in my life."

"I think we're lucky to have found each other. We have a beautiful and powerful son, and no matter what happens, I will never regret a moment of it. Love you," she whispered.

"I love you, too, Frost."

Xander watched her fall asleep and smiled at the sound of her deep, even breathing. Soon, he followed her into oblivion.

Chapter Fifteen

Frost

Silas was close to a month old and of course, Liv had been right about everything. Silas grew no faster than a typical human baby, meeting the standards and weight that Liv tested him for once a week for the last four weeks, but his powers had grown exponentially. His barrier could stretch as far as he wanted it to, and nothing could get through the barrier. They had tried gasses, liquids, and even tried to break through it using explosives. Despite the fact that the experiments scared the shit out of Frost, Silas thought it was hilarious. Especially when they shot at it and Axel had tried to break it down using an ax. Nothing worked.

But he also had a strength that scared her a bit. He could easily move an object, like a heavy dresser, by using only a small amount of force.

That had taken everyone by surprise.

He'd been sitting on the floor of the bedroom—Frost had figured it was easier to change the diaper there considering he'd been busy burrowing under the blanket in the first place—when he placed his hand on the dresser leg and sent it skidding five feet against the wall. After that, she became more aware of where he was and who he was with. She would have to kill Ax if he taught her son anything dangerous.

And they had learned, over the last few days, that Silas could, if he wanted to, manipulate emotions. When Kane had been thinking about his mate, the one who had been killed several years previous, Silas pushed feelings of happiness and love to him, until Kane hugged the boy close. He used it sparingly, usually when someone was frustrated or angry, and he was quick to make them happy. And being only a month old, happiness was at the top of Silas's lists of emotions he believed everyone should feel.

They had also learned a bit more about Anzû and his company. He had thirty or so shifters on his payroll, mainly hiring men out as temporary bodyguards or the type of muscle that paid well. The men weren't loyal to Anzû, he was a means to an end. Ghost hadn't recognized any of the shifters as asking for a job with Dark Company.

Anzû and his cronies had gone quiet, not issuing any threats or contacting them in any way, which led the assassins to occupy their time with Silas. Each day, their little man grew and learned. And with each of the assassins, he had his own routine.

Jade loved to play peek-a-boo with him, laughing whenever she came in the room. Silas loved Ax in his lion form. He said he was fuzzy and comfy, something which Ax tried hard to fight, but gave up when he saw it made Silas happy. Whenever he was with the assassins and he grew tired, you could find him curled on Ax's paw, fast asleep.

When Silas sat in his bouncer, the one she bought for him, he would roll a large ball of string around the room for Hunter's panther to chase. He brought it back after swatting it around for a few minutes, and after dropping it on Silas's lap, and Hunter would nuzzle her son until he laughed. Hunter would purr loudly whenever that happened.

Liv loved talking to him through their mind link, both silent and intent on their conversation, sometimes with Seth joining in. Liv told Frost that she showed him pictures of her past, like her sister Molly. She also told Silas how important he and his mommy were, and that she was so glad his daddy found his mommy.

And the vampires would take turns as they ran around outside, with Silas wrapped in their arms. He loved their speed and their agility. They would tell him about their lives and what they enjoyed about being immortal and Silas would always listen with rapt attention. And Kai, who Frost had believed to be closed off, spoke most to Silas about everything that happened in his life from the moment he became an immortal to when he met Liv. He had a gentle nature with her son and she loved him for it.

But Xander's time with Silas made her smile. He read to Silas every night before bed, always choosing a different book and reading until Silas fell asleep, only to pick up where he left off the next night. Xander had expressed the need to sleep during the night and be awake during the day. He said Silas was a growing boy, but again, Silas had differing thoughts on the matter.

He wanted to be around both his vampire and shifter aunts and uncles, so he compromised. He would go to bed around three in the morning, having already adjusted to it when he had been born, and then wake up sometime the next afternoon. He was always rested, and because he was a baby, still took several naps during the day, usually when the excitement became too much.

Most nights Xander would tuck Silas in his crib, but soon, Silas would call for Xander until his dad lifted him from the crib and laid him between them. He would be spoiled, but she couldn't bring herself to care much about that.

Silas had his blood taken about two weeks after his birth, and that's when they learned that he healed faster than a typical immortal. Liv confirmed that he was full immortal shifter and when the time was right, his body would allow him to shift.

Mommy.

She blinked and turned to Silas with a smile. She lifted him from his crib as he rubbed his eyes, still waking from his nap. "Yes, baby?"

You won't leave Daddy or me, will you?

She kissed his already longer white hair. "No, baby, I would never leave you and Daddy."

Xander wrapped his arms around her waist and pressed her back against his chest. "We'll always be together, little man. No one is going anywhere."

I...I heard a strange man's voice outside. He said that Mommy was his and that he would kill everyone to get her.

Frost held Silas tighter as Xander tightened his hold.

"Did you talk to this man?" Xander's voice was tight with tension.

No. He wants to hurt my family.

Curses flooded her mind and did nothing to quell the panic inside her. Soon, the panic transformed into pure rage and she handed Silas to Xander.

Give me a minute, will you?

Xander nodded and pulled Silas tighter to him, explaining through their mind link that she was fine.

She stalked out of the room and spotted a wooden training dummy in the hallway. Not even questioning why it had been placed there, she closed her fist and centered her punch in the middle of the main support. With satisfaction, she heard the creak of the breaks that spread through the rest of the stand until it collapsed.

Do you feel better?

A bit. Frost reached for Silas and kissed him on his cheeks before nuzzling his neck with her nose, all while Xander laughed.

__Chapter Sixteen__

Xander

Xander was horrified that Anzû had gotten close enough for Silas to hear his thoughts, but not close enough to trip any perimeter alarms. But they had just discovered a huge advantage: Silas could hear him.

Xander had been able to communicate with his fellow assassins for years, but he'd forgotten how much effort it took to open a mind link with someone new. No one wanted their mind invaded, even if they could only listen to what he had to say and not hear every thought, and even by someone they trusted.

So when Ghost had introduced the idea, everyone scoffed at it. Ghost reasoned that it would make them a better team and they all eventually acquiesced. Training to mind link had been more exhausting than combat, weapons training, and tracking combined. He would rather be out in the cold for weeks on end, tracking a target that was well trained in diversion and evasion tactics, than mind linking with another.

With Frost close to his side and Silas in his arms, they headed downstairs to relay this new information to Ghost and the others. When he had finished explaining, some of them, like him, were pissed that Anzû had tried to get so close. Most of them thought it was great that Silas could hear the fuck, giving them a bigger and hopefully ultimate advantage.

Jade and Ax walked in and they looked as though they had gotten their asses kicked.

"The assignment was compromised. There were several shifters laying in wait, and it was a hell of a fight."

Ghost left the room, probably to call his contact and ask about the specifics of the contract.

As Liv pulled out one of the first-aid kits, one of many that were stashed around the house, Frost started to clean Ax's injuries.

"Do you want me naked?" Ax asked her. "I'm willing to do this, for you."

Frost wiggled her eyebrows and Ax smiled, a knowing smile that relayed hope that she would say yes. "No, I'm good, big man. I've seen it before."

Silas laughed aloud and everyone turned to him. Then laughter filled the room as they fell in love with Silas's light sound.

But when Ghost came back in, they all sobered. "The contract didn't come through normal channels, so I guess that Anzû wanted to test us and see how prepared we were. He faked the location and target. From now on, the contracts will be scrutinized and rechecked by me. Anzû and Nightfall have been put on a watchlist and he'll never work as a contractor again."

There wasn't anything really left to do, not until they could fill Kai and the rest of the vampires in on their plan.

Hungry.

"Can I feed him and then take him for a walk around outside? It's a nice day and I want to spend time with my favorite little man."

Xander glanced at his mate and smiled at Jade, nodding his thanks. Then he turned his gaze to his mate. He had been missing her over the past month. Although he agreed with Liv when she had recommended that Frost take a break before they made love again, it had driven him crazy now that he abided by her suggestion. He had kissed her and touched her, but refrained from making love to her.

But it had been worse for Frost during the time they abstained. Her hormones went haywire after the birth, and more than once, she had almost talked him into making love to her. When that didn't work, she had gone for the all-out seduction. That had been the hardest experience of his life, resisting his mate, the one who called to him in every way. She hadn't tried again when she realized how serious he was as he conveyed his worry about her health, but he would pull her close every night and tell her how much he loved her. That seemed to satisfy her, for a bit. But today she was given the all clear.

Frost caught his eye and tilted her head up the stairs. Xander gasped when an image flashed of him pinning her to the door with his body as he drove into her, a pure look of ecstasy of her face.

Xander reached for Frost's hand and they darted upstairs, closing and locking the bedroom door behind them. He blew out a breath when they hadn't run into anyone in the hallway. There was always someone roaming about.

"It's been too long."

"I know, sweetheart, and I'm sorry."

She jumped in his arms and their lips met in a scorching kiss. Her hands ripped his shirt so that she could get to his skin. "I've missed this."

His hands traveled over her as they made their way to the bed. "Are you truly ready to make love?"

When she growled and pressed her lips to his neck and sucked, he tilted his head back and moaned at the sensations she drew from him.

"Fuck, sweetheart, I need you."

"Finally."

As he went to lay her on the bed, she managed to flip them until his back was pressed against the mattress. Without missing a beat, she latched onto his nipple and sucked, darting her tongue against the sensitive flesh and he growled at the sensations that went straight to his cock. She reached for his belt and loosened it, before snapping open the button of his jeans, and then placed her mouth on his stomach and pressed down, her tongue tracing around his navel. She drew his jeans and boxer briefs down, and licked and nipped at his hipbones, not leaving any inch of his skin untouched.

Soon, she reached for the base of his pulsing, swollen cock and swirled her tongue around the head, drawing curses and moans buried deep in his chest. He moaned her name in such a ragged and torn way that he scented her rush of arousal immediately. Instead of climbing on top of him and taking her pleasure, she swallowed his cock and listened to his breathing stutter out of his chest. His spine tingled with unspeakable pleasure, and he knew that he needed to be inside her or all of this would be over before it began.

Before he could speak or move, she reached up to cup his balls and he wasn't prepared for the stroke of pleasure that licked up his spine.

"Fuck, sweetheart, I need to be inside you."

He flipped her onto her back with the utmost care, before he kissed his way down her breasts, savoring the taste of her swollen nipples. He kissed down her stomach, nipping at her hipbones, before he finished with kissing the top of her mound. He listened to her heavy breathing and without hesitation, licked a swath from her entrance to her clit, wrapping his tongue around her sensitized bundle of nerves. He sucked it into his mouth as he inserted one finger inside her. Both of the overwhelming sensations had her coming over his finger and down his hand.

He surged back onto the bed and kissed her, both losing themselves in the sensations.

Please, Xander. Fuck me. I can't wait any longer.

Xander, with more care than necessary, going by Frost's warning growl, slid inside her and once their hips were pressed together, they

139

both let out a sigh of pleasure. Xander pulled back and thrust in, losing himself in her scent and the sensation of loving her, his mate. He drove hard as she encouraged him with her moans and pleas, both through their mind link and aloud. Soon, they both released and for a moment, everything fell away until it was just them, loving in the most elemental way.

When he caught his breath, he rolled to his side and pulled her close, and when he glanced at her, he noticed that her eyes had changed, again.

"Your eyes…they're aqua."

Frost laughed. "Each time we make love, it seems as though we discover something new. I couldn't be happier."

Xander relaxed back and reached to open his bedside drawer, pulling out a black box.

"I know this isn't traditional, and that's something that suits us to a T, but will you marry me?"

He opened the box, revealing a band. The smaller diamonds circling both edges were accentuated by the brilliant blue-green stones that wrapped around the entire band.

"Yes, Xander. I would love to marry you. But let's have a quick, small ceremony. I only care that I'm your wife."

Xander kissed her. "Anything you want, sweetheart."

Over the next few hours, they made love and talked about their future. Even though they had never been so happy, there was a small niggle, knowing who was coming for them and their family. Whatever happened, Xander knew that they would get through it, together.

Chapter Seventeen

Frost

Over the past few weeks, Silas had been working on turning off other's thoughts whenever he wanted to. At just three months, Silas had explained that voices seemed to push their way into his brain without having a filter or a way to block them. They could have been miles away and all he could hear were voices and thoughts, and he needed to control what he let filter through. Xander had been helping him, and this morning Silas announced that he was able to successfully stop the thoughts and voices completely. Unless someone spoke to him through their mind link specifically.

Because they learned that Silas could hear thoughts over a great distance, and now block them, he wondered whether Silas could drop the shield he learned to use to block other's thoughts and voices and project those voices into someone's head. Xander explained it as an overwhelming force of thought that would paralyze another's mind because they wouldn't be able to block the thoughts from their own mind. Silas had just finished learning how to shield himself and Frost wanted him to take a break, but he insisted that he could do it. He'd been partly successful and told them that he didn't like it, forcing thoughts into another's head, and she had put a stop to any training.

Silas was a happy baby, laughing and loving everyone in his family. He sensed emotions, and after a mission, he would push happiness and contentment into which ever assassin had come back from assignment. It would be subtle and non-evasive, but soon, happiness spread throughout the house and Silas would smile at everyone as he joined in.

A week after Xander had proposed, they were married in a small ceremony in their living room. They had been married by the same ordained minister who had married Kai and Liv and Seth and Aubrey. He had a warm, friendly face and although she had been nervous during the ceremony, hearing the minister's soothing voice and holding Silas close calmed her a great deal. Xander held his arm around her waist during the ceremony and smiled at her, but she had blanked most of it out when she met Xander's gaze. She allowed herself to be lost in his light-blue eyes.

After, they had a celebration and Silas loved it when Xander danced with both of them most of the night, happiness radiating off him in waves. The day had been perfect.

Silas had woken a few minutes before and she fed him, but soon he asked her if he could sit with Jade, Ax, and Hunter. Before long, the three assassins had shifted and were rolling around the carpet, nuzzling Silas and loving it when he laughed aloud.

Xander wrapped her in his arms, setting his head on her shoulder as they watched their son. "What are you thinking about?"

"Nothing much. I'm happy with my family and my mate. Enjoying the fact that Silas will grow up like a somewhat normal baby and we'll get to have a lot of time with him."

"You're not worried anymore?"

She shrugged. "We can prepare and train as much as we want, but we don't know when that asshole will strike, and I'd rather not worry about what might happen and just deal with it when it does."

"That's what I'm afraid of. Him taking Silas."

She turned around and pinned Xander with her gaze. "If he comes anywhere near Silas, I will rip him limb from limb until there is nothing identifiable left."

Xander cursed under his breath as his eyes widened. "I wouldn't fuck with you. But sweetheart, your eyes are glowing, flashing between blue and green."

Silas fussed as he sat near the other shifters. Frost scooped him up and made herself calm down as she hugged her son.

Why are you mad, Mommy?

"Daddy and I will never let anyone hurt you. I was just thinking about what we would have to do to keep you safe."

I know. But Mommy, I can protect myself.

"What do you mean, baby?"

Silas closed his eyes and scrunched up his face, and within seconds, she held a little snow leopard cub in her arms. He was pure white and when he looked up at her, his unique eyes twinkling at her, she pressed her forehead to his and smiled. "My little man is brilliant."

He rubbed his head underneath her chin and she laughed.

"Oh, come on. It's only me who takes a half a decade to shift?" Ara growled and Silas chuffed.

Frost sensed that Silas wanted a chance to roam around the house now that he wasn't restricted by his human baby body, and set him down. With sure movements, he joined the others. Xander shifted without a thought and tickled Silas with his nose. When Xander dropped onto his back, Silas climbed all over him, happy that he was able to play. And Frost was ecstatic for her son. She wasn't really surprised Silas could do it; he was a determined little immortal.

Liv sat down beside Frost, and soon Jade, still in her red fox form, crawled onto Frost's lap and settled down. Frost smiled when she realized how far they came since the first time she growled and threatened Jade. They all had, and just like Xander, she thought of everyone as her family.

"What's it like, being a mom?" Liv asked.

"It's exactly how you feel about everyone in this room. You feel proud that they are capable and strong, that they are happy and know that they can come to you anytime, just to talk or ask for advice. But you worry about them and pray for them to be safe, healthy, and happy. You don't want them to grow up and not need you anymore, but know that it's a part of life."

I wouldn't mind finding a mate, but I'm not holding my breath. Jade sounded a little sad, not that she would ever admit it.

"You, my favorite redhead, will find someone when you least expect it."

They watched Silas lope around, easily finding his balance as if it were second nature, as he rounded Xander before he leapt on him. Frost smiled at Silas whenever he glanced over at her, but before long, Silas slowly walked over to her and she picked him up. Jade got up and said that she was going to change.

Mommy, I'm tired.

Frost nuzzled him close. As his eyes finally closed, he shifted back and she rushed him upstairs to dress before he became too cold. Once dressed, she put him to bed and waited for Xander to lock up the house, knowing that their little man would be out for the rest of the night. He didn't dream or send out random thoughts as he slept.

When Xander entered the room, she pulled him close and kissed him deeply. They didn't need to speak. Xander understood exactly what she needed whenever she needed it, and she loved him for it. She navigated him toward the bed and pushed him onto his back. Over the next few minutes, she proceeded to worship his body, uncovering every inch before pressing her lips or running her hands over him, loving the sounds she drew from him.

Every time they made love, it felt new and exciting. Still awed that she got to touch and love this man made her movements desperate as she kissed down his naked chest. She sucked on his nipples and licked the ridges of his stomach, smiling into his skin when he moaned, which sent shafts of pleasure straight to her core.

When she reached his hard, leaking cock, she swallowed all of him. Well, as much as she could take. She savored the salty taste and something she always identified as purely Xander.

Bringing him to the brink of an orgasm, she pulled her mouth from him and squeezed the base of his cock to stave off his orgasm. She threw her leg over his thighs and crawled up a few inches before she sank down on his cock without hesitation. She threw back her head and moaned as he filled her.

"Frost." The way he said her name sent ripples of pleasure throughout her body.

He gripped her hips and when she rose and lowered herself to take him deeper, he thrust his hips up, driving even deeper inside her. The feeling left her panting and begging for more.

"I love you. You are my everything, Xander."

"Fuck...I love you, too, sweetheart. So much more than I'll ever be able to express."

At his words, she threw back her head as she clamped down on his cock, feeling his hands tighten on her hips a split second before his cock flooded her with his hot release. She shivered from the sensations she would never grow tired of, and before long, she came down from her high and dropped onto Xander's chest.

"Too...tired...to move."

Xander reached for the comforter and pulled it over both of them, before he banded his arms around her and pulled her face into his neck. She fell asleep with the warmth and love coming from her mate and husband.

Chapter Eighteen

Xander

Xander and Frost were out on their daily trek around the woods with Silas. Jade and Ax had decided to join them. Because their little man had been shifting, he needed to expend the energy that came along with shifting and growing stronger every day. So at night, after dinner, they had taken to exploring the mountain. He and his son were in their snow leopard forms.

The summer had passed fairly quickly and their little cub was five months old. His shifts had become easier and it didn't tire him out as much as the first one had. They worried when Silas slept through the night and most of the next day. But shifting took a lot of energy and they monitored him throughout the next day, and he soon recovered.

Since the weather had settled from warm to cool evenings, they enjoyed their walks more and more. They couldn't wait for him to see snow for the first time.

Anzû had been silent since the call Ghost had received and as far as they could tell, stopped his push to take over Dark Company. Xander had hoped that he'd given up, but he knew better. The reason that their friends had joined them on their nightly ritual was because Ghost knew better as well.

And the sick part, despite the looming threat, was Xander had never been happier in his life.

He walked closer to Frost and he loved how she ran her fingers through his fur as they both kept an eye on Silas. He understood why he had lived so many years alone. He had to wait for Frost to come into his life. He remembered the feeling of being alone. But every morning, he woke up next to his wife and mate, and with their son sleeping next to them, content and dreaming happy dreams, he knew he was the luckiest man. And with his extended family vowing to protect them, as he would protect them, he knew that they could handle whatever Anzû threw at them. But he wished he would hurry the fuck up with his plans.

Xander laughed as Silas had a burst of energy and ran around the trees, darting in and out, before looping back to keep his parents in sight. He had developed speed in his leopard form, only with the occasional stumble. But as he grew more confident in his abilities, he shifted often. In his human form, he was stuck with someone holding him, and he liked that when he was tired or wanted to cuddle with Frost, but he couldn't crawl at his young age and this way, he was free to run. Xander couldn't fault him for that.

Xander was alerted to the change in their environment when Silas stopped running. His ears perked up, and his furry head tilted a bit to the right, as if he were listening to someone speak.

Two men are talking. Maybe more. No, wait. Not talking, thinking as they track something.

Frost stood by Silas as Jade and Ax turned in the direction of where Silas had heard the intruders' thoughts. Xander put himself in front of his family. They readied themselves for an attack whenever the men came into view.

They've gone quiet. Their minds blanked.

Silas jumped into Frost's arms, but the moment she straightened, they all heard a low whistle of something they couldn't identify, heading their way. With horror, Xander watched a dart pierce the soft skin of Frost's neck. Her eyes widened and she put Silas underneath Xander before reaching for the dart and pulling it out. Her eyes drooped and she fell unconscious.

Stay under me, little man.

He managed to break her fall and laid her gently on the grass using his head, before he stood in front of her, standing guard, ready to kill anyone who came close.

Silas, I need you to go to Jade and keep close.

Okay, Daddy.

Silas quickly made his way to Jade and Xander felt that he had erected a barrier around all of them the moment he reached her. It had been just in time, because the shifters emerged from the bushes at full sprint, their sights set on grabbing Frost. They slammed into the barrier and it knocked them back on their assess. They looked around, confused. They stepped back to regroup.

Silas, keep the barrier around you and Mommy only, okay?

Silas sent out a wave of anxiety that Xander recognized. *Don't worry, little man. We will be fine. I promise.*

He sensed more than spotted the shield move away from Jade, Ax, and himself. Without waiting, they sprung at the intruders, pushing them deeper into the trees and away from Silas and Frost. He didn't want Silas seeing what he had to do.

Jade opened her mouth, showing her sharp teeth and howling, effectively distracting the two shifters, while Ax came up behind them and swiped at both with his gigantic claws. As one of the men started to run away, Xander jumped on him and wrapped his mouth around his neck, not hesitating to clamp his jaw closed and effectively breaking the shifter's neck. Not hesitating, he bit clean through the shifter's throat and spine, only satisfied when his head detached and rolled away from his body.

"Wait, wait. I have a message. You have to let me live," the last intruder pleaded.

Xander chuffed and growled, showing all of his teeth. They planned on kidnapping Frost and relaying the warning. Their confidence was their downfall. But Silas had saved his mom and now this fucker wanted to negotiate. These guys would pay.

Fuck the warning, Xander communicated to Ax. Ax swung his big paw down, effectively decapitating the second intruder before he had another chance to speak.

While Ax and Xander buried the two, Jade went back and watched over his family. He knew he should have felt a pang of remorse for killing the immortals, but they advanced on them with violence first, and their deaths had been the price they had to pay.

Xander finished up. He and Ax walked back toward the others. He was proud of his son. Silas still had the barrier up.

Okay, little man. Ready to go home?

Yes. Silas sounded so lost.

When Silas dropped his barrier, Xander shifted back and picked up Silas, who had also shifted back. He gently lifted his wife and walked them both back home. He tried to rid himself of the anger and adrenaline coursing through him, but he knew it wouldn't be worth the effort. It would dissipate when he got his family home and safe. Ax and Jade sensed this and kept quiet.

He rushed through the front door and carried them up to their bedroom, laying Frost on the bed and then Silas, who cuddled up against her side. He dressed Silas in pajamas and covered them both. Xander leaned toward Frost and could smell the scent of the tranquilizer she'd been shot with. He closed his eyes and reassured himself that she would be all right when he heard her steady heartbeat and rhythmic breathing.

Ghost walked in as Xander pulled up his jeans and reached for a shirt. Silas blinked open his eyes and held up his arms for Ghost to pick him up, which he did. Silas, with his talents, played back the entire event, minus what happened after he and the others disappeared through the trees. When Silas had been through it all,

Ghost kissed his head and gently placed him back against Frost. Both men watched as he cuddled in the crook of her neck.

He's waiting for us to slip up. His only objective was to kidnap Frost. We had to kill them.

That's understandable. Don't be so hard on yourself. They tried to kidnap your mate. You did the right thing. Ghost squeezed his shoulder and the last of Xander's adrenaline washed away.

Ghost left them to be together, and Xander cuddled next to his mate, careful of Silas between them. Unable to stand the distance, he pulled her closer and Silas blew out a breath, a wave of happiness that both his parents lay next to him.

Xander shivered in fear at how close he was to losing her. If it wasn't for Silas, they would have most likely succeeded. With his adrenaline completely drained, but with the horrifying thoughts swirling around in his mind, he fell into a fitful, yet exhausted sleep with his arms wrapped tightly around his entire world.

Chapter Nineteen

Frost

Frost awoke slowly and wondered why her head felt detached from the rest of her body. Her thoughts floated around in her head, and no matter how much she had concentrated on pinning one down, they managed to flitter away the moment she had some semblance of recognition. Instead of targeting one thought, she asked questions and she hoped that she could find enough strength to answer them.

Am I hurt? No, not hurt. The only problem was that her head was fuzzy with something other than sleep.

What do you remember last? Huh. That took a little longer to remember. Silas. Silas and Xander were running around the mountain, darting in and out of the trees as they chased each other. She—no Xander—wrestled with Silas in their leopard forms until...what? Silas...something that had to do with Silas.

Her throat constricted with panic as she tried to pull the memories from the back of her mind. It took her a few minutes to push away the dread that came with her thoughts, enough so she could concentrate on the full recollection of their time playing in the trees. But all she could see was Silas, his pure white and tiny form, tripping from time to time as he tried to keep up with his dad.

There. What was that? Frost watched in her mind's view as Silas paused and quirked his ears up to hear a conversation. No, not a conversation; thoughts, he said. Others' thoughts, who were closing in on their positions.

Why?

That she didn't remember. She reached for Silas. *Did she drop him? Hurt him?*

Again, despair locked down her body and froze her mind at the thought of her son, their son, hurt or worse because she couldn't protect him. *Xander.* She knew that Xander would protect him, both of them, with a ferocity that would scare other immortals.

Concentrate, Frost, for fuck's sake.

A little swell of pain, in her neck. She remembered that. Silas—she had moved Silas underneath Xander so his dad could protect him, but after that, nothing but darkness. Darkness and the bleakness of not knowing whether her family was still alive.

She felt tears pour down her face, something that she couldn't have prevented, even if she wanted to. Her muscles were slow to respond; she couldn't even clench her hands into fists. *What the hell was in that dart that struck her?*

Dart—there was a dart that she pulled out of her neck. She remembered glancing at it as though it were the cause of all the trouble in her life. And because she couldn't move, was she being kept—by Anzû? No, she had to get out, to get back to her family. But as much as she struggled, nothing would move. She tried to pry open her eyes and yet, nothing.

Her chest heaved up and down with her fearful breaths. Without a way to relax her body with the thoughts and the imaginings of what had happened to her family, she blacked out.

***

Awareness slowly seeped in and she couldn't remember for a split second, where she was or how she got here. The panic that she had felt and that made her pass out seemed dampened by the thoughts pinging around in her mind. She could think, make connections, and she wasn't sluggish. But instead of getting excited, she knew that she would have to assess her current situation.

Her breathing slowed as she listened for any movement anywhere around, and she could distinctly hear two different breathing patterns close to where she lay. She sensed no danger, so she relaxed a bit more. She took a deep breath and inhaled the familiar scents of her son and mate in the same room, and she unlocked the rest of her muscles and opened her eyes.

Xander's arm lay around her waist, his hand splayed around her hip and holding her close to his side. His head was buried against her neck, and that's when she spotted Silas. He was curled in between them, touching both of them in his sleep as reassurance that his parents were safe and sound.

And suddenly she was pissed. Silas had witnessed the attack on her and even worse, she had no idea what happened to him. *Did they attack him as well?* She couldn't contain the growl that escaped her throat. In the same moment, Xander's eyes popped open and met hers; his widened when he spotted the fury in hers.

Did those fuckers touch Silas?

No, no sweetheart. He protected you while Jade, Ax, and I took care of them.

They're dead then? Frost was pissed enough at that moment that she wouldn't have minded a shot at them. Not that she knew how to kill anyone, but for putting Silas in danger, she would've found a way. The throbbing in her head became more pronounced.

Are you okay, sweetheart?

Yeah, just a headache. I think it's a leftover product of being tranquilized. Earlier I couldn't even move. How long have I been out?

He glanced at the clock and looked back at her with wide eyes. *It's been eight hours. The tranquilizer should have burned up in your system within an hour. They must've upped the dose and miscalculated. If you were still a human, it would've killed you.*

What happened? She glossed over the dose. A headache was a small price to pay considering what could have happened to her family.

Xander relayed exactly what had occurred, leaving nothing out, even how the shifters had died at their hands. But the message threw her. Why would he leave a message with Xander if their goal was to kidnap her? She smiled down at her son, proud of their little man. He'd kept his cool and despite the worry that he must've been feeling, he did exactly as his daddy instructed.

Why would they try to kidnap me? It makes no sense, after all this time, unless he really wanted Silas and thought that kidnapping me would give him an advantage. I hope he comes back, because he wouldn't survive the encounter.

Xander captured her lips and kissed her until her breathing became erratic and she had forgotten her anger that was replaced by lust for her mate. When he pulled back, she ran her fingers through his hair. The devastated look on his face caused her heart to squeeze painfully in her chest. She never wanted to be a liability to Xander, but last night, she had become one.

I've never been so scared. When I spotted the dart in your neck, I almost had a heart attack.

I'm sorry. I didn't—

No, sweetheart. I wouldn't change a moment between us. It's him and we have to destroy him, because he's never getting another chance at you or Silas.

I believe you. I would never leave you two, you are my world. Anzû has had too many failures—he's going to make his play soon. After five months of waiting and now losing two of his men, he's going to be looking for payback. And he's not exactly stable, so when he does attack us, we'll have to be prepared for underhanded tactics.

Xander beamed at her and kissed her again, before he broke off. She pulled Silas onto her chest as she laid her head on Xander's shoulder, needing reassurance that her family was fine and Xander wrapped his arms them and squeezed them close. She lost track of time as they listened to Silas's dreams that he projected out to them. They were happy, full of color and featured those he loved most in the world. Xander and Frost were always together and Silas would focus on them more often than not.

Unfortunately, her stomach rumbled and then she remembered she had missed dinner.

"We should go eat. He'll be fine up here," Xander reassured her.

She nodded and they moved an exhausted Silas to his crib. As soon as she lay him down, she felt his barrier surround the house, protecting everyone in it. She smiled at her little man and kissed him on the head, before she turned and reached for Xander's hand, linking their fingers together, and headed downstairs.

Grateful that the house was crowded, they walked toward the delicious smells and noticed that the table was scattered with platters of food, enough to feed an army, or just enough for nine hungry shifters. When she sat, Ax pushed a plate full of pot roast and vegetables over to her and then Xander. She nodded her thanks and dug in.

"You scared us, Frost." Liv's voice shook as she spoke.

Frost pulled the small vampire in for a hug and rubbed her back in reassurance that she was okay. Liv held on tighter than normal for a few seconds, before standing up and smiling at her, blowing out a breath of relief.

"I'm sorry. I heard it long before it hit, but I couldn't recognize the sound. Trust me, they won't have a second chance to try it again."

Xander conveyed Frost's thoughts about Anzû ramping up his plans, and the assassins started to bandy around ideas. But Frost was too hungry and pissed to care about what the plan might be. She piled seconds on her plate, not eating like this since she'd been pregnant, and felt a pang of sadness. She missed Silas so close, so protected.

But her little man had powers that she would've never dreamed anyone could possess. And when her thoughts centered on Silas's talent to hear someone's thoughts for a great distance, she spoke aloud.

"What if we get Silas to alert us when Anzû is near? That way, we could ambush him before he gets anywhere near the house and we could still have an advantage to kill him before he comes near Silas."

"You're a bit scary when you want revenge," Hunter mumbled.

Her answering smile was all the response he received, and it wasn't a nice smile. If she were honest with herself, she knew that she would go after Anzû herself if she knew where she could find him, with or without the help of the assassins. He shouldn't have gone after her when her son had been near, and that would be his fatal mistake.

"We'll talk to Silas when he wakes up. But if he alerts us, then will have to be ready in moments. We don't want him to be able to locate where any of us live in case there's a small chance he escapes. He seems exactly like to type to abandon his men if it means he gets to save his own skin," Xander pointed out.

"I'm fine with killing Anzû and anyone else who seeks to destroy us, but I would like to give the other immortals an opportunity to run if they want." They all agreed with Ghost, that unless they continued fighting long after their leader was dead, they would let the others be.

They continued planning and Frost zoned out, pulling a piece of chocolate cake her way, grateful that she could eat chocolate again. But the assassins looked at her as if she might be pregnant again, and she dispelled them of the notion.

"Nope, no glowing of the skin during sex, and Ax, we've had a lot of sex. And since I'm eating chocolate, I know I'm not pregnant. This stuff made me sick to even smell it when I was pregnant. Xander and I haven't discussed the possibility of another child, but we want to have a chance to spoil Silas rotten without the thought of our upcoming deaths hanging over our heads. But you guys will be the first to know if it happens. Happy?"

They all nodded and went back to their various discussions. When she was finished savoring her cake—and it was good cake—Xander pulled her aside. "I want you to be with Silas and Liv inside the house when we go after Anzû."

She stared at him, her teeth clenched and her hands fisted at her sides, waiting to see whether he would come to his senses and take back his words. Unfortunately, that didn't happen.

"You're out of your mind, mate of mine. I will be by your side when we take him out, and Silas will be protected inside this house. He's not getting a second chance to live after what he put Silas through last night. Do you think I would really sit back and allow

Anzû to have a chance to hurt you as well? And see how I'm trying really hard not to curse here?"

Xander threw back his head and laughed. He pulled her close and kissed her, despite the audience in the room having gone suddenly quiet. "And that's why I love you. You won't take any shit, not even from me. And I'm sorry, I should have known better."

Mommy!

With one last kiss on Xander's cheek, she rushed upstairs. When she spotted Silas standing at the railing of his crib, she smiled at him. She had tried to let go of the anger and the hatred she felt toward a man she'd never formally met, but she must've had some residual anger because the moment he saw her, Silas started to cry. He hadn't cried, ever. Not when he'd been born, or when he'd tripped as a cub and taken a tumble down the last three stairs and into the living room.

"Hey, little man, everything's okay."

Her words made him cry harder. She had always called him her little man, and he would smile and hold his arms out for her, but seeing her incapacitated must have truly scared him.

Lifting him in her arms, she cradled him close to her body as she turned toward the rocking chair in the corner and gently sat. She tucked his head in his favorite spot, underneath her chin, and she started humming to him. Something that always calmed him.

Silent tears poured down his little face and splashed against her neck and at that moment, her heart broke for her little man. She should have never put him in that situation to begin with and she hoped that soon, she would have the opportunity to kill Anzû.

When his tears slowed and he fisted his little hands in her shirt, tangling them together, she rubbed his back and spoke.

"It's okay, baby. Mommy's here and she's fine. She'll always be fine. I promised you that I wasn't going anywhere, and I will keep that promise, okay?"

She didn't really expect him to reply, so she stroked her fingers through his hair and the other hand continued to rub soothing circles on his back. She resumed her humming. She usually hummed to calm him when he had too much energy to fall asleep, the sound relaxing him in a way that had become their constant since Silas first shifted. And every night she loved to hold her baby, feeling as close to him as she could get, as he clung to her.

In the early morning, he finally calmed down enough that she knew he would need to see Xander to truly feel safe. She made her way downstairs and grabbed the other rocking chair in the house. When Xander spotted them and ran his hand over Silas's back as she had done, Silas heaved a big sigh and blinked open his eyes to stare at his daddy.

"Hey, little man. We have a plan that I think will work to keep the bad man away from Mommy. Do you want to hear it?"

I don't want Anzû to know about Silas. Even though he knew I was pregnant, I don't want him to know anything about him, even his name.

With this plan, sweetheart, he'll never know.

Silas rubbed the sleep from his eyes with his two little fists, blinking and becoming aware of everyone in the room. Instead of sending out waves of happiness, he was oddly subdued.

"I'm going to feed him, and then you can talk to him."

Frost decided that he would be hungry, just as she was, and took him to the kitchen. Silas had chosen carrots this time, along with apples for dessert, and as she fed him, she kept making silly faces after he swallowed and before long, he smiled back at her.

You know I love you and Daddy more than anything else in the entire world. Right, baby?

Yes, Mommy, I know. But...

He won't have a chance to do anything like that again. Daddy has come up with a plan to make both of us safe and once the bad man's gone, we won't have to worry about him or anyone else again.

Okay, Mommy. I trust you and Daddy.

Good, let's eat and then go talk to Daddy.

Silas ate the rest of his dinner and when she cleaned his mouth and then picked him up again, she smiled when he cuddled close. She walked back in the living room and let Xander know that Silas was ready to hear what he had to say.

"Okay, little man. We know you're special and could mind link and hear anyone's thoughts, but I want you to push all of your family's thoughts into Anzû. That way, he'll have so many voices in his head, like you did before you learned to control it, that it would drive him crazy and we could get rid of him. He won't know where the thoughts are coming from, and he might think that Mommy has become more powerful than he ever imagined, which will make him pause for a moment."

"Since he won't know where it's coming from, he won't suspect Silas. But are you sure that this will work? He seems to know things that we don't. Maybe this isn't such a good idea—"

Mommy, I want to help.

They discussed it for a long while and decided that any offense would give them the advantage in the long run, and this way, Silas would be safe in the house under his impenetrable barrier. Silas agreed that he would work to center all thoughts into one mind. He was happy that he would be included in the plan that would "make the bad man go away", and so when it was settled, he sent a wave of happiness and contentment throughout the room. All they had to do now was wait and see.

<u>Chapter Twenty</u>

Xander

Xander had demanded that Frost train with him after they'd come up with their plan. She had insisted that she would accompany him and the rest of the assassins when they confronted Anzû and his merry band of men, as Frost had taken to calling them. At first, he had restrained himself because the last thing he wanted was to hurt her, and then have to explain to Silas what happened to his mommy so soon after the incident, as they referred to it.

Silas kept close to both of them since then, and although they loved getting more cuddles from their son before he grew out of showing his affection for his parents, they had been afraid that he wouldn't get over the trauma of what he'd seen. But days had passed and he was back to his normal self.

Of course, Frost took to training like a natural. When he taught her hand-to-hand combat, she had kicked his ass more times than he could count. She understood and repeated the moves so quickly, he started to wonder whether she had faked her inexperience. When he mentioned this, she scoffed and charged him. He started to realize that as determined as she was to protect their son and him, his mate had proved, again, that she was capable of anything.

But now she seemed as though she reveled in kicking his ass. *A lot.*

During the moments that they didn't spend with Silas, or training, or helped Silas relax his mind enough to push thoughts that weren't his own into one brain, Xander would find a way to get Frost alone. They had made love in every room in the house—well, the ones that had locking doors—and couldn't get enough of each other. It seemed as though they made love as if it were the last chance they would have to become so intimate, but to Frost and Xander, it was the norm.

Kissing would lead to touching, touching would lead to ripping their clothing off, and soon they would make love until they both screamed their release and clung to each other. They hadn't left each other's sight for very long, and he loved that his mate craved his touches as much as he craved hers.

During the moments where they were getting their breathing back to normal, they had talked about the possibility of other children. Silas would like to have a sibling and the thought of another baby who had Frost's gorgeous features and maybe his shocking hair made Xander want to try again. But Frost was right. Not until the threat had been eliminated.

Mommy! Daddy!

"Yes, little man, we're right here."

No, he's here. Outside. Right now.

"It's on!" Xander shouted and the others knew what he meant.

For the past few days, other immortals from Dark Company, the one's who preferred lives to themselves, had joined the already established group after they had learned from Ghost about Silas, the immortal born into their group. They had been just as taken with Silas as anyone who met him, and their son was happy to have so many more aunts and uncles than he previously thought. And having badass assassins, who preferred to be brooding loners, melt at the sight of his son made Xander smile for days. And because of Silas, they had stuck around and added numbers to fight against the threat.

Frost cuddled Silas and kissed him on the forehead, before Xander did the same. *It'll be okay, baby. We promise.*

So they gathered. Kai, Reaper, Ara, Seth, Aubrey, Jade, Hunter, Gunnar, Ghost, Axel, Kane, Thomas, Isaac, and thirty others, along with Frost and himself, marched out the door on that cool September night. He locked the house down before he spoke to his son, who had gone straight into his Aunt Liv's arms as soon as he heard Anzû's voice.

Barrier up, little man. Round the entire house. Protect yourself and your Aunt Liv, okay, baby?

Okay, Daddy.

They could feel the impenetrable barrier surround the entire property, shimmering against the surface of the house, before Xander pulled Frost close to him. They could feel that a large group advanced toward them. With one look back at the house to make sure his son was protected, he and the other's faced toward the sound and braced himself for the fight that was to come.

Anzû came into view, looking rougher than the picture of him depicted. His brown hair stood straight up on end, as if he'd been in the habit of pulling at it. His eyes, wide and crazy, glanced around at the immortals, including several vampires, all gathered against him. He paused, not speaking, only looking for a long minute, before his eyes landed on Frost who leaned against Xander's side.

"Give me Frost. She's a defective shifter mutt anyway. She'll never be able to make a good mate—she can't even shift. I'm willing to accept that she is damaged and accept her anyway."

Xander growled and it was joined by snarls and hisses from the rest of his immortal family. The shifters who flanked Anzû took a step back, letting the assassins know that they weren't as dedicated to Anzû as they were to their own survival. Maybe that would work to their advantage.

Anzû lifted his brow when the protest ended. He truly believed that Frost would join him or they would be willing to sacrifice her without a second thought.

Well, fuck that.

Son, now!

Silas's hard work had paid off when they watched as Anzû grabbed his head and dropped to his knees, keening loudly at what must have been a painful rush of thoughts inside his own head. But as they had practiced, the thoughts increased tenfold as all of the Dark Company assassins started to mind link with each other.

The others in Anzû's group had no clue how to continue without instructions from their leader, who was now writhing on the ground, screaming in pain. They kept glancing at Frost, thinking that she had the power to do this. To add to their beliefs, her eyes moved over the group that followed Anzû and she lifted the side of her lip in a part snarl, part nasty smile he knew that would scare the shit out of them.

One of them stepped toward Frost, and Xander's arm banded tighter around her waist as the chorus of growls and snarls stopped his progress cold.

Anzû screamed in pain as he surged to his feet and staggered toward Frost. "Why are you doing this to me?"

Frost's smile widened, but she continued to stand there next to Xander, silent.

Anzû pushed past the pain and swung his fist toward them as he stepped forward, and he struck her in the face with his closed fist. Frost was stronger than he gave her credit for, because she didn't move an inch when his hit landed on her cheek. Xander's hand moved as Anzû's did; he wrapped his hand around the immortal's forearm and crushed it when he closed his fist and twisted. Xander yanked Anzû closer, dislocating his shoulder in the process. His hold on Anzû gave Frost ample time to return the punch to his jawbone and they all listened to the satisfying crack of his jaw breaking. The smile never left her lips.

Xander landed a blow on Anzû's nose a moment before Frost's foot landed square in his chest, launching him back as the blood splattered against his face and down his shirt. He landed in a heap several yards from them.

"This man you believe to be your leader has no chance of taking over Dark Company, despite what he might have told you. He lied to you, probably about everything since you've been hired, which is why you aren't loyal to him. If you still want to fight, you could stick around and get a firsthand demonstration of how a real team of immortals, both vampire and shifter, work together. But I wouldn't recommend it." Ghost's voice rang out in the darkness.

Several had done the smart thing and turned around, heading out the way they came in, but fifteen stood with Anzû. Xander, not giving them a chance to talk or back out of the fight, made a split-second decision and attacked. He kept one eye on Frost as he incapacitated those in his path, and soon, the fighting behind him started in earnest.

What became apparently clear in the next few minutes was that these men had no real training of any kind. They had tried for a few minutes to fight without weapons, but punch after punch was landed on their core and their face. They had tried to retreat enough to regroup, which none of the assassins would allow them to do. They had kept the group separated from one another, taking away their advantage of fighting as one, but one of them pulled a gun and shot Hunter in the shoulder. The panther howled in anger and lunged for the one stupid enough to shoot him, and effectively ripped his head off.

Xander easily disarmed the shifter he'd been fighting against, but the man pulled out his knife sheathed against his ankle and managed to stab him through the thigh. The pain only managed to piss Xander off. With one punch to the immortal's face, he crushed the bones in his face. The impact managed to separate the immortal's brain stem and he dropped to the ground, forgotten.

The vampires had taken to biting the shifters they had fought, effectively swamping their system with vampire venom, which was deadly to the shifter. They dropped as soon as their bodies were infected and they moved on to the next shifters. Kane, Thomas, and Isaac had stuck together and were taking out the majority of the shifters, while Kai preferred a hands-on approach. That vampire was scary as hell when he fought.

Ax, Gunnar, and Jade stuck together. Jade took the other shifters' feet out from under them as they preferred to stay in their human forms rather than shift. When they lost their balance, Gunnar and Ax would go for their jugular and either break their necks or rip out their brain stems.

Frost stuck close to Xander, and she preferred to fight with her tactical knife that she had taken a liking to during training, and watched as not one of her opponents got a strike before she severed an artery or ripped their hearts out.

Xander became distracted when he had two shifters rush him. He took one out with a quick step forward, striking him in the nose with the palm of his hand and driving the bone straight into his brain and stepped over him when he fell to the ground, dead. As he glanced around, he noticed that he had moved too far away from Frost. When he saw movement to his right, he glanced up and watched in horror as Anzû spun Frost around and wrapped his hand around her neck and pressed her back against his chest, the knife pressed close to an artery in her throat.

"Let…her…go. I won't ask you again." Xander's voice had never taken such a deep tone before. He was both frightened and determined to kill this motherfucker once and for all.

Anzû flinched and Xander realized that he could sense Frost's distress, and of course, amped up the thoughts pressing into Anzû's head. He continued to bombard him with thoughts until Anzû spoke.

"I will saw her head off her body and kill your abomination of a child if you don't get that brat to stop with the assault." Anzû closed his eyes as he spoke.

Everything in that moment slowed to a standstill. Anzû knew about Silas, knew about his powers, while he had his mate under knifepoint and threatened to kill her. *What the fuck have I done in this life that was so bad to deserve this shit?*

His eyes flashed to his mate, hoping to convey to her that he would get her out of this situation, but instead, he watched her face morph into something that, frankly, scared the living shit out of him.

At the same moment her eyes sparked with pure rage, she knocked the knife away from her neck with a simple brush of her hand. When it was free of her neck, Frost leapt into the air and before Xander had a chance to blink, her shift had already begun. By the time she flipped around and her head snapped down toward Anzû's exposed neck, she had shifted fully. Her bright-white fur along her body was contrasted by the black pattern that ran over her head and down to her muzzle of her snow leopard form. The brightness of her fur lightened the darkness that surrounded them and they could see her movements clearly.

A loud growl escaped her throat as her mouth opened and her large white teeth flashed, a second before they clamped down around Anzû's neck. Her teeth sank into his throat as she bit down and he could clearly hear a gurgling sound as her mouth tightened. Anzû had been taken completely by surprise and didn't even have time to shift, before he dropped to the ground. The look of utter astonishment broke over his face, before her teeth cut through the soft tissue of his neck and severed his spine. The look of surprise was permanently etched on his features as his head rolled off his body.

Silence surrounded them at the sight before them. Then, all at once, there was a mad scramble for those who had survived their encounter with the assassins, once they heard their leader's neck snap. They let the others go without thoughts of pursuit. Hopefully they would remember how easily they were defeated and if they were smart, wouldn't be stupid enough to challenge them again. Right now, though, Xander couldn't care less about them.

Xander approached Frost, and when he met her gaze, he sucked in a breath because her green eyes looked back at him. He remembered how green they were when they first met. The mix of blue was absent in this form. But what surprised him was the tears that formed in her eyes as she glanced down at Anzû and then back up to him.

"Sweetheart, you did what you had to do to protect Silas. There is nothing to be ashamed about or to feel bad about. We knew that he would never stop coming after us if you hadn't taken care of him. And he would have done much more than threaten our son if we gave him the chance."

As Xander mentioned their son, Frost looked at the house.

"Silas would want to see you as a snow leopard. By the way, you look ferocious with the black markings around your eyes and forehead. It's absolutely beautiful. But let's clean your muzzle before heading back to the house. Silas is fine. I hear him humming contentedly. Liv must be reading to him."

Frost chuffed at him and he smiled.

He proceeded to wash the blood off her muzzle, making sure there wasn't any trace of it, before they walked up to the house. The others trailed behind, glad to give them time together. As soon as Xander opened the door, they rushed up the stairs and peeked in the door. Liv had Silas cradled against her neck as he stared intently at the book in front of him. But when Liv paused to turn the page, Silas glanced up and his smile widened as he got his first good look at Frost as a snow leopard.

"Mommy pretty."

At five and a half months, their baby had just spoken, aloud, his first words. Both of them were completely stunned when they turned to look at each other. Of course, their son was remarkable; they shouldn't have been surprised.

Frost sauntered closer.

Silas reached a hand out and patted the top of her head. *You did good, Mommy. He wanted to hurt Daddy and all of my aunts and uncles. You couldn't let that happen.*

Frost chuffed.

I love you, Mommy.

I love you, too, baby. And Daddy, too.

Xander smiled when Frost finally relaxed.

I love you, too, sweetheart. With all that I am.

Chapter Twenty-One

Frost

Frost was rolling on the floor with Silas in the living room, both of them in their snow leopard forms, as Silas gave her a ferocious growl before he pounced on her. She absolutely loved being able to play with her son as Xander had all those months. This time, Xander stood nearby, leaning against the doorjamb of the kitchen and watching over them with a smile on his face. She had noticed that since Anzû had been taken care of, Xander was a lot happier, and not due to Silas's influence.

"Has there been any play against us?" Xander asked.

Ghost shook his head. They didn't expect anyone to try to infiltrate Dark Company after she had effectively killed Anzû in front of those men who had survived, and would most likely go and tell the tale. She had quickly moved past the guilt, thanks to her son, and was grateful that the threat to them and the others had passed. For now. Power always attracted those who didn't have it and Ghost and the assassins, although they didn't flaunt their place in the world or within the government, would always be under threat because it came with the territory. But if another play ever did come, they would all be ready for it, including her.

Frost had been curious about her sudden ability to shift and had asked Xander about it one night after they'd tucked Silas into bed.

"Your baby was threatened. Although you hadn't shifted yet, instinct took over and allowed you to shift because you were protecting Silas. Nothing is stronger than a bond between a mother and their child, and because you would do anything for him, you shifted."

Xander always gazed in her eyes when she shifted, and he told her it was because they had turned to her original green color when she was in her leopard form. Although Liv had some answers when it came to Frost's unusual transition and pregnancy, there were still unanswered questions as to how half-shifters, half-humans worked. She suspected that each shifter or vampire mix were different, but essentially the same in the fundamentals of being able to conceive. Until they found another, they wouldn't have the answers they craved.

Frost had transitioned back when she became too tired to support her snow leopard form, and she had been worried, although silently, that she wouldn't be able to shift again. She froze when Silas had asked her to go for a run, all three of them, but with a little concentration, she felt her body shift, and within seconds, she glanced down and spotted her white paws. Of course, Ara had cursed, rather loudly. But Frost reminded her that she could boil the blood in a human body within seconds and she cheered up significantly.

Frost had told Liv that she could experiment on her blood now that she shifted, drawing from her as much as they wanted, but she didn't care that she was unique in the immortal world. She had her husband and her son, who were both happy and healthy, and that's all that mattered to her.

Frost chuffed when they were joined in the living room by Ax, Hunter, Gunnar, and Jade in their lion, panther, gray wolf, and red fox forms, and roughhoused with Silas as Frost looked on. She had been lying on the floor when Ax rolled onto his back and pressed his huge, soft head against Frost's neck and took a deep breath. Of course, Xander growled at the lion-shifter, who continued to ignore him.

I don't mind, love. I'm happy to be part of this large family. Plus, he doesn't mean anything by it. I think that he's waiting for his own mate, although he would never admit it aloud. But sometimes I see him with a sad look on his face when no one is looking. Plus, I think he might be a little scared of me and getting close is his way of proving he's brave.

Xander doubled up with laughter as he clutched his stomach and waved off the others who looked at him. Frost had learned that family was important. Yes, she loved her parents, but her childhood had been a lonely one, all by herself. Some of the assassins thought of Silas as their younger brother and even started referring to him as that, and Frost loved it.

She nuzzled her son, who lay breathless against Hunter's paw, and told him that Xander and she would be back. Silas chuffed and turned back to the group he was playing with.

With that, she turned toward the stairs and glanced back at Xander, before she ran up the stairs. She sensed more than heard Xander follow her upstairs. As soon as he closed and locked the door, Frost shifted back and tackled Xander onto the bed.

Their lips met and he devoured her as he would every time they kissed. Her body flared and she could feel her core flood with wet heat, and forgot everything but the sensations that only Xander could draw from her. When they broke the kiss, they took deep breaths and she moaned at the sight of his lowered lids, his swollen lips, and his chest heaving up and down as he breathed.

"I love you."

"I love you, too. The luckiest day of my life was the one where I found you. Everything in my life has meaning, because of you. Because of how much you love me and I love you."

Xander had believed—according to the conversations that he had with Ara, and Ara had conveyed to her one night when Xander and Silas had gone out for a run—he believed he missed his life mate and over the past year, had given up on finding her. Although others could see how much it hurt him to think about, Xander was the first one to support the others as they had found and fallen in love with their own. But Ara had encouraged him not to give up, because as she told him, love takes time. Frost had hugged her tightly after Ara had relayed all of their conversations.

And her relationship with Xander was easy. As easy as breathing. He introduced her to their large family, gave her a son whom she adored and loved, and loved her more than their entire existence. Almost as much as she loved him. She showed him every day, in all ways that she could, that she would never hurt him and she would spend the rest of their existence proving it to him.

As they stripped and jumped on the bed, Xander brushed her hair away from her face before he cupped her cheek. They stared into each other's eyes, communicating without uttering a word. She pulled him in for a kiss, a scorching one that had her begging for his cock. When he slid in and their hips pressed together, she let out a moan and wrapped her arms around his strong back, her nails biting against his skin, which caused his hips to jerk forward.

"Yes, like that, just like that."

They lost themselves in the sensations. He drove forward, again and again, as she matched his thrusts with her own. And like each time, her first orgasm took her by surprise. She clenched down on Xander as he pushed through, her sensitized flesh gripping as her entire body shivered from her release.

When he rolled on his back and brought her up to straddle his hips, she had recovered enough to slide her hips back and forth, grinding herself on him as he reached for her hips and squeezed. She loved when he did that, anchored himself to her as she continued her movements, this time adding a lift, before she slammed back down onto him. She squeezed his cock and loved his moan that vibrated though her.

"Xander, again."

She had just enough time before her next orgasm washed over her and she leaned back. He had bent his knees and caught her before she fell. At this angle, he drove up into her as he held her hips in place, and soon, his loud groan echoed throughout the room.

"Come inside me, Xander. I want to feel you."

"Frost, oh, fuck." With that, he threw his head back and she felt his cock swell as he emptied deep inside her. Her body clenched down around him, and when she opened her eyes, her skin flashed with a glow, before it faded.

"Did you…"

"See that?" Xander finished.

Unable to hold herself upright, she dropped down onto Xander's chest and kissed his skin when he wrapped his arms around her and tightened his hold.

"Every time, you take my breath away, sweetheart."

She chuckled against his skin, before she rested her head on her hands and stared into his eyes.

"Happy?" Frost kissed him.

"Very."

Mommy! Daddy! Where are you?

They both laughed. Although he could speak, Silas preferred to communicate through their mind link. He struggled to speak complete sentences and became frustrated, so he just reverted back.

"He'll be six months in a week," she reminded Xander.

They dressed quickly and when they opened the door, they almost ran into a smirking Jade with a wiggling Silas in her arms, whose face bloomed into a smile when he spotted them. Xander reached for their son, nuzzling his neck with his nose, and Silas laughed. Before Frost could blink, she had Jade in her arms, hugging her.

"Could we get ice cream now? Silas has been talking non-stop about ice cream for over a hour and now I want some."

"Yes, Red, we can get some ice cream."

Jade beamed at her before turning on her heel and leading them back downstairs. Frost found herself dishing up ice cream for all those who could eat and she paused on the last bowl for herself, taking a quick look around and smiling at her family crowded throughout the house. Xander sensed her happiness and wrapped his arm around her and pressed his warm chest to her back.

"It's funny how quickly everything can change. And with you, Silas, and our crazy family, I will always feel lucky to have found you."

"Me too, sweetheart. I love you."

"I love you, too."

The End

Look for Jade (A Dark Assassins Novel Book Four), arriving October 31st, 2017!
To be the first to know when the next Dark Assassins novel will be released, and discover my other releases by joining my monthly newsletter at http://www.valerieullmer.com/newsletter/

ABOUT THE AUTHOR

Valerie resides in Denver, Colorado with her husband and their dog, Maddie. While she had been interested in writing a romance novel for years, it wasn't until she wrote her first book that she really became hooked, and now she can't stop. She has notebooks full of ideas, and she plans to write most of them in the years to come.

When she's not writing or learning about the craft of writing, she can be found surfing the internet way too much, watching Investigation Discovery and thinking that her neighbors are up to no good, and finding new ways to get her husband to laugh.

Please contact Valerie at valerie@valerieullmer.com or visit her website http://www.valerieullmer.com.

Printed in Great Britain
by Amazon